USA TODAY BESTSELLING AUTHOR

Dale Mayer

HEROES FOR HIRE

DAKOTA'S DELIGHT: HEROES FOR HIRE, BOOK 9
Beverly Dale Mayer
Valley Publishing Ltd.

ISBN-13: 978-1-773360-45-4
Print Edition

Books in This Series:

Carson's Choice: Heroes for Hire, Book 28

Dante's Decision: Heroes for Hire, Book 29

Steven's Solace: Heroes for Hire, Book 30

Boxed Sets and Bundles

https://geni.us/Bundlepage

About This Book

Welcome to Dakota's Delight, book 9 in Heroes for Hire, reconnecting readers with the unforgettable men from SEALs of Honor in a new series of action packed, page turning romantic suspense that fans have come to expect from USA TODAY Bestselling author Dale Mayer.

When a young woman darts into traffic and into Dakota's path, life takes a dark turn for both of them.

Bailey, recovering from the loss of her husband, retreated from life. Going to work and coming home was the extent of her days and weeks. Until she walks into work early one morning, witnesses a murder and flees into traffic, nearly getting killed.

The near death experience awakens the spark of life inside of her. So does the man in the car. A different kind of a spark.

For her safety, Dakota persuades her to move into the compound with him and the rest of the Legendary family while they track down the killers.

Bailey is forced to accept Dakota's help. But can she stay safe long enough for the police to track down the killer? Or is the man who almost ran her over going to steal her heart?

Sign up to be notified of all Dale's releases here!
https://geni.us/DaleNews

Chapter 1

DAKOTA LANGUOR DROVE his big SUV through the intersection, his list of things to do today long. He was often the one to go into town, depending on who was available and what else was going on. He did the job cheerfully, knowing it gave him a chance to get out. He loved everybody he worked with, absolutely adored the women there, but, for him, it got to be a bit too much at times.

He wasn't used to living and working in the middle of a large family. And that was definitely what Legendary Security had become. He was good with that, but sometimes …

Saul was his best friend, and now that he'd found Rebel and she lived in town, the two of them were fast becoming another case of a live-in couple. Dakota knew Saul had discussed with Rebel about moving into one of the apartments on the compound.

Eight apartments were being rehabbed for company employees. Dakota doubted that would be enough, considering the speed with which Levi was filling up his company with some of the best damn men Dakota had ever been privileged to work with.

Dakota sped down the highway. He might stop for lunch or coffee, but he'd knock the things off his list like a pro—fast and efficient. Most of today was picking up parts and pieces that had been ordered from various warehouses and stores. Food had to be picked up too—that was always fun as Alfred's list would be huge. The good thing was, he had phoned in the order, and it was paid for, ready for loading by the time Dakota got there.

Considering Levi had so many jobs on the go right now, with men coming and going on a regular basis, Dakota liked this diversion. Saul had just headed out to a job in Alaska and was always happy to go off on missions, but, at the same time, he would miss his sweetheart. To think how Saul and Rebel had worked out as a couple was amazing. Dakota was happy for his buddy. Saul hadn't been looking for a relationship, but, when it came, he'd certainly recognized its value and gone with it.

Dakota wasn't sure he'd have the same foresight. He'd never been married, and his years in the navy had shown just how difficult that life was on his friends' relationships. In Dakota's case, having been a SEAL and going off on dangerous missions had been very hard on his former girlfriends. And he never knew when he would come back, *if* he would come back. He figured it was easier on everybody if he didn't give his heart away, so there would be less hurt all around. It was not that he wanted to be single all his life, and he certainly had a less dangerous lifestyle now, but it was still the same kind of work, and he was gone on a regular basis.

Plus he'd moved to Texas for this position. He didn't want to do anything to mess it up. He really enjoyed the people he worked with. He'd worried that, when he left the navy, he'd feel this huge apprehension, fear of losing that sense of brotherhood. But, as he had hooked up with Levi almost immediately, Dakota had experienced a renewed sense of kinship and a sense of belonging. He loved his new life.

The fact that almost everybody here, living on the compound as Levi's people did, was involved in a serious relationship made being single a bit awkward. But Dakota was okay with that because it was comfortable and maybe because he was even a little envious.

He'd watched Saul and Rebel come together, spark back and forth off each other, before settling into something that was almost like a lock and a key.

He hadn't really expected that to happen to Saul. They'd been best friends forever. Saul had had several serious relationships during that time. Dakota had thought some of the women were perfect for his buddy. But none had ever worked out. Rebel had been completely different. And yet perfect. Considering how quickly Saul had clicked with Rebel, Dakota had to wonder if he could have that something special too. Not that one could plan for that.

Dakota's huge fear was that the perfect woman would walk by and that he wouldn't recognize her.

As he came to the outskirts of the city, he checked before changing lanes and then took a right at the next intersection. The best way to get through this long list was to be efficient about which places he went to and in what order. He stopped off at the first warehouse and picked up several parcels that had come in for Levi, loaded them into the back of the SUV, pushing them to the far corner and packing them in tight. By the time he got home today this vehicle would be stuffed, so he had to pack for maximum usage of his space. Plus the perishables had to be the last ones in and the first ones out.

At the mechanic shop, he picked up a few parts and

pieces Stone and Merk had ordered for a couple of the rigs. The good thing was, everything was done on credit, and Ice paid all the bills. Dakota didn't have to deal with the money issues. Originally, when Ice and Levi had first started the company, apparently finances had been very tight, but, now that money flowed freely and the company turned a profit, the co-owners were building up a lot of their inventory, improving on the medical clinic and rehabbing many of the apartments. Levi had inherited the huge compound from a family member, and, ever since they'd moved in, the place had been under construction.

Of course Alfred was a godsend. He ran the house and commanded the kitchen, where he created delicious meals for the entire compound single-handedly. There had been a lot of discussion about bringing in an assistant for him. Instead everyone just pitched in and helped alongside him. Nobody let him do dishes anymore, even though he protested mightily. But there was no need for that, as about thirty people hung around or lived in the place most of the time. Not all the bedrooms were full yet. But it must be getting close.

Once the apartments were completed, Dakota knew a lot of the couples would move into those spaces. That would change things too. He didn't know how the meals would work at that point, but he figured it would probably be up to the individual couples. Some were so busy they'd appreciate offered food, and others may like to cook special dinners themselves. Dakota wasn't sure how Alfred would handle life then, but, like everything else, after a few growing pains, he'd settle into a rhythm that would work for everyone.

Dakota made two more stops, cheerfully knocking them off his list. Just as he pulled away from his fourth stop, the rain came down. Within minutes the downpour was so extreme that he could barely see through the windshield. He reached an intersection and was about to pull through as various vehicles slid out of control, hydroplaning—the flooding in the streets was bad already.

He decided to get out of these main traffic areas. Side streets would be less dangerous. He took a right and then a left, and, as he turned right again, he peered left, then right. Both clear, he hit the gas.

A woman darted into his path. He yanked the steering wheel sharply yet still felt the bump as he hit her.

"Shit!"

He pounded on the brakes; the truck slammed to a stop. He shut off the engine, opened the door and ran outside. The woman leaned against his truck, staring at him with a dazed look in her eyes.

"Oh, my God. Are you okay?" He jogged to her, automatically assessing her condition. He found no blood, and she appeared to be standing on her own.

She looked up at him and said, "I'm ... I'm fine."

He shook his head. "No, you so aren't."

She gave him a brief smile and said, "Yes, I am."

And with that she took a deep breath, almost as if she would go underwater, and she bolted. Down the street he watched her gait, seeing a limp on her left side and how she held herself with her arm wrapped around her chest. He knew that, although she wasn't badly hurt, she was still injured. He hopped back into the truck, turned on the engine, completed the turn and went after her. She bolted up an alleyway. He followed.

He felt terrible. He hadn't seen her before driving into the section, didn't know where she came from until she was in the roadway, but he wanted her checked over by a doctor. It was like she had blasted from the darkness. He came up to the alleyway but saw no sign of her. He drove around the block and came down the alleyway from the far side, hoping to catch her coming out at the other end. He proceeded slowly around the corner. No one was there. No doorway was open.

Dakota passed by a door where a couple came out, laughing and joking at the rain, racing to get under cover at the store on the corner. Dakota pulled off to the side and parked. He opened the car door and raced to the door the couple had come out of. And stepped into the kitchen of a small restaurant.

The chef turned and frowned at him. "Use the front door," he barked.

"Sorry. Did you see a young woman come through here just a few minutes ago?"

The chef motioned to the front of the restaurant. "Yeah, she's in there."

"Thanks." He gave himself a quick shake, ridding himself of the effects of the rain.

"Remember the front door next time."

"I will, thanks."

He made his way to the front, passing a waitress carrying a tray of empty plates. "Sorry."

He stopped to check out the boisterous atmosphere. He didn't know this restaurant at all. It looked more like a small café, diner style. He walked past the tables, looking for the woman who'd run away from him.

Up ahead, sitting at a small table for two with a glass of water in front of her, was the woman he'd hit with his vehicle. He quickly sat down in the chair across from her.

She jerked back and stared at him in shock. And then slowly recognition kicked into her gaze, and she sank back into her chair. "I said I was fine."

He shook his head. "You're limping and holding your side," he said, leaning closer. "I can't in good conscience let you walk away without having a doctor check you over."

She shook her head and bitterly said, "I can't meet my deductible, so it wouldn't matter if I *was* injured."

He reached across and picked up her hand, holding it gently. "I'll take care of your bill. I just want to make sure you are fine."

She studied him intently. Then, as if she wanted to say something but couldn't let herself, she snapped her lips together and pinched them closed.

He sighed and sat back. "Are you always so stubborn?" he asked lightly.

"No, only when men track me down and scare the devil out of me."

Her phrasing was interesting. The waitress walked over just then with a coffee carafe and two cups.

As she was about to leave, Dakota said, "Would you bring us a menu too, please?"

With a bright smile the waitress disappeared to get the menus.

He looked over at the woman. "At least tell me your name. I'm Dakota Languor." He reached out his hand across the table to shake hers.

She shook his hand and said, "I'm Bailey Hoskins."

"I like it. It's different." He tossed it around in his mind and then shrugged. "I like unique."

"It is different," she said gently. "That also made it diffi-cult to grow up with. Kids had a problem with my name being different. So the kids deemed me different," she said quietly. "It doesn't really matter in what way."

"Were you bullied growing up?"

She shrugged. "No more than anybody else I suppose, but I certainly got my fair share." She studied his face, then dropped her gaze to his broad shoulders.

He knew what she saw. He was the epitome of the all-American boy—muscled, tanned.

Then she smiled. "I guess you weren't though?"

"Never twice by the same person." His tone was flat. He had no patience for those who were busy mocking others. "I've always been a straight player. And I don't waste my time with those who aren't."

"So why are you here wasting time with me?" she asked in a half-mocking tone.

"Because I don't even know what happened," he admitted. "Not only were you running into a street without looking, but you were running away from something. I've seen too many cases, where a woman ran in terror, to not stop and ask if she needs help."

She settled back into her chair, about to protest, when the waitress returned and placed a menu in front of her, handing the second menu to Dakota. "I'll be back in a minute."

Dakota nodded his thanks and raised the menu, but over the top he watched her slowly stirring her coffee.

She dipped her spoon in the cup and pulled up a bit of the dark liquid, taking a sip and grimacing.

He grinned. "Not much of a coffee drinker?"

She shrugged. "Not a whole lot, no."

He nudged the sugar and cream toward her. "Maybe try it with one of these."

She studied them both and picked up the cream and poured in a decent amount.

He went back to reading the menu and decided the daily special, a chef's burger, was perfect right now. He glanced over the menu at her. "At least let me buy you lunch."

The offer seemed to startle her. Finally she nodded. "Thank you. I'd appreciate that."

"Did your shirt or pants get damaged when you hit the vehicle?"

She glanced down, brushing at the moisture that clung to the material. "No. I doubt it."

He motioned at the menu in front of her. "Pick something."

She put the menu up between the two of them as if a barrier would help him go away. He wouldn't do that, but he could understand her wanting to hide behind something.

He was patient as she studied her lunch options. If she was hoping to outwait him, she was out of luck. He wasn't letting her from his sight until he had answers.

Finally she put the menu off to the side. "I'll have a green salad."

The waitress, as if seeing her actions, walked over to take their orders. He wasted no time in asking for two large burgers, fries, and a green salad for her. They went over the extras he wanted on the burgers, and finally the waitress collected the menus and walked away.

She stared at him. "Did you even listen to me?"

"I listened. Obviously you need more food than a green salad. And, even if you're only a little bit hurt, your body needs to heal. You were still in shock when I arrived, and that means you need food, real food."

"I'm not in shock," she protested.

"Yes, you are. Your hands are still trembling. You're still wrapping your arms around your body from being cold and wet. If something happened to you before we ran into each other, literally, that's just added to the effect. What were you running from?"

She turned to stare at the pouring rain outside the window. "I'd just left the office and was heading to the bank. It's a fair distance, so I cut through alleys to get there on my break. In a hurry, I wasn't watching where I was going," she said in a low tone. "It's not your fault."

"And yet I feel like it is," he said gently. "I did not stop in time. And it really bothers me to think you might end up walking out of here with what appears to be a minor injury but could end up becoming much worse."

"I'm fine. I have no pain anywhere."

"I'm glad to hear that."

"But you really don't believe me, do you?"

"It's not that I don't believe you, but, when somebody's in shock, they aren't always aware of how badly injured they are." His lips quirked. "Until later when it's often too late."

She slumped back into her chair and just stared out the window. But she did pick up her coffee cup and took a sip. The cup trembled in her hand.

He wanted to reach over and hold her hand steady, letting her know she'd be fine—he'd make sure of it.

She jerkily moved her hand forward and finally set the cup down again. Even getting a little bit of coffee into her seemed to help. It put some life back in her eyes.

"Are you ready to tell me what happened before we collided?"

She shook her head. "I have no intention of telling you anything."

As he suspected. Something had terrified her into running, and that's why she'd ended up in the road where she shouldn't have been. He certainly didn't let himself off the hook. His reaction should've been faster. Yet the rain was so heavy, it had been hard to see.

"Do you live in Houston?" he asked.

"Yes, I've been here for a few years." Giving him a small sideways look, she asked, "You?"

"I've been here a couple months now," he confessed. "A friend of mine and I moved out here for jobs with the same company."

"Oh, that's nice that the two of you came at the same time."

He shrugged. "We work for Legendary Security. We were both in the navy, so leaving at the same time and moving here was actually a good deal on both our parts. We've been buddies for a long time, so we didn't really want to find jobs across the world and have to start over without anybody there beside us."

"Having friends makes everything easier." She reached out a hand and added a bit more cream to her coffee.

He frowned as he noticed her translucent skin and the big bruise on the back of her hand. "You look like you never eat."

She raised her gaze, studying him for a long moment. "I'm getting better now."

"Were you sick?" he asked, his tone sharp.

She shook her head. "Emotionally traumatized. I lost my husband eighteen months ago. I came close to fading away. I just didn't care anymore. But I turned a corner a few months ago, and I've been slowly regaining my strength."

She picked up her coffee and took several more sips as

she again stared out the window.

He knew she wasn't seeing anything out there but was staring more into the long line of years behind her. "I'm sorry. That's very difficult."

"It was very difficult. He was sick. When he went in for tests, they found he had stage four cancer. He was gone within six months. There was just no time to even adapt, to get through treatment or even try to fight. He was there, and then he was too sick to be anywhere but in the hospital. He was moved to the hospital so damn fast, and we just didn't realize how quickly everything would be over." She shook her head, clenching her fingers together. "We'd only been married six months before he got really ill."

"At least you had those first six months," he said gently.

She gave him a tremulous smile. "It took me a long time to see that. But you're right. Still, when you lose somebody, it's hard not to rail against the injustices of the world, not to cry and not to be angry because you're the one left behind, the people you love all gone. I dived into my work and ended up volunteering after-hours. I did everything I could to work myself to the bone, so I couldn't feel. To just delay getting home and trying to sleep at night so I could get up and do it all over again. I lost a lot of weight, and it wasn't exactly a healthy lifestyle. But it took quite a while for me to sleep and even more time to get up without tears in my eyes."

"Even eighteen months isn't very long for grieving."

"No, but it's long enough," she said. "I realized quite a few months ago I had to do something about my downward spiral, and Rick would be very upset with me if he knew I was letting myself decline to that extent. He always asked me to take care of myself. It's not that I wasn't able or capable, it just never occurred to me. I'd go without several meals and not really notice, and then suddenly I'd be super hungry and have to eat."

"Regular meals are necessary to keep your energy up."

"Why would I want to keep my energy up? I wanted to come home and to drop off to sleep until the next day. It was only through sleep that I could forget the pain of what I'd lost."

Just then the waitress walked over with two large platters.

Dakota looked at the stacked burger with appreciation. He'd have to remember this place. "This looks great," he said.

He studied the platter in front of Bailey. The burger was just as big as his with a decent size salad too. He picked up his burger carefully—large enough that he needed two hands to hold it—and took a big bite. Real meat, barbecued perfectly on a grill, just the way he liked it.

Together they munched in silence, enjoying the hot food and being inside the warm café. When he finished his burger, he turned his platter and offered her some fries.

She shook her head. "It'll be all I can do to eat my own."

"I suspect you didn't have any breakfast this morning, did you?"

She shook her head. "No, I had breakfast a long time ago." She sighed heavily. "You probably shouldn't be talking to me. Or be seen with me in any way."

He raised an eyebrow in question. "Why's that?" He popped a french fry into his mouth and chewed.

She shook her head again but wouldn't explain.

He knew there was more to the story, but he wasn't exactly sure how to get it out of her. "What are you running from?"

She gave a broken laugh. "That's why you shouldn't be talking to me. For all I know, you're in trouble now."

"How?" He tried to keep his tone gentle and undemanding, but no way was he letting her off the hook with this. He needed to know what had happened.

She shook her head and continued to eat her salad. The waitress came back and topped off her coffee.

He let her eat in silence for a few more moments and then said, "Tell me what is wrong."

She looked at him. "You can't fix it. And I'm not putting anybody else in danger."

"What danger?"

She just shrugged but kept silent.

"Remember I work for a private security company? Remember I was in the navy? Handling danger is what I do. I help people in trouble."

"Maybe, but you do it for money, and that's not something I have. And this is too dangerous, even for you."

He sat back, shifting sideways on the chair, figuring out how to get her to open up. He was more a "if the hammer didn't work, then bring in a sledgehammer" type of guy. But that approach didn't work well with women. He needed to find the key to helping her relax.

"Money isn't the issue," he said gently. "If I can do anything to help, you need to tell me."

This time her headshake was emphatic. "Thank you for lunch," she said. "I have to go to the ladies' room. Excuse me please."

She stood up, grabbed her purse and walked past him. Having sat for the last hour, her body was stiff, and he could see her limp was more pronounced. He swore under his breath. He really needed to look at her leg. She was also slightly hunched over, and he knew that was to protect her ribs. It was possible she had cracked one or two. He hoped it was just bruising instead, but he knew even that would take a long time to heal. He watched until she walked past the rest of the tables and went into the women's bathroom. Then he waited.

INSIDE THE BATHROOM Bailey stared at her reflection in the mirror, hating to see the huge bags under her eyes and the fear still lurking in the background. "What the hell has happened to my life?" she whispered to her reflection.

She used the facilities and turned back to the sink, washing her hands as she embraced the heat of the water. She was so cold inside and out, and her body was stiff and sore. She certainly didn't blame him. She'd run smack into his vehicle. A damn good thing he wasn't going any faster and had deflected the impact, as she probably would've been killed or severely injured at least.

She took a moment to brush her hair as she gathered her thoughts. She didn't know what to say or what to tell him to make him happy enough to leave her alone. He was just a little too determined to keep her close. She was hoping she'd escape from the restaurant without him seeing her leave. It meant sticking him with the bill, but, since he'd offered, she didn't feel guilty. Not to mention he had ordered three times the food she would have.

A knock came on the door. She quickly dried off her hands, wiped her face, tossed the paper towel into the garbage can and opened the door. She smiled at the middle-aged woman and stepped out. Then she searched the restaurant, looking for a way to get past Dakota. A large noisy crowd of office workers came in as a group. They walked past him, heading for a table between the two of them.

Quickly she joined the crowd, eased to the outside of the group, getting past Dakota's table, and made it to the front door. She opened the door and slipped outside.

The rain had eased up, which was a good thing. She was still so very cold. She needed to get home, and she needed to get home now.

She turned the corner at the closest intersection and crossed the road. Just as she stepped up on the far side, a hand grabbed her elbow gently. And she knew without turning around it was Dakota. "You should let me go."

"We'll go around to my truck, then I'll take you home. You shouldn't be walking around in the rain when you're injured," he said firmly.

She shook her head. "I live a few blocks away."

"Good, then it won't take very long to get you home."

She couldn't protest without causing a lot of attention, and that wasn't something she wanted.

She let him lead her around to the alleyway and help her into his large black SUV. Inside she was dry and warm and comfortable. She settled back into the deep seat and buckled up.

When he got in and turned on the vehicle, he pivoted and looked at her. "Where are we going?"

She gave him a few simple directions, and, a couple minutes later, they pulled up in front of her apartment building, with visitor parking on the street. He turned off the engine, hopped out and came around to her side. She wondered at his sense of chivalry, that he opened the door and reached up to help her down. Maybe he was just afraid she would sue him, when, in truth, all she wanted was to be left alone.

He led her up the apartment building steps. "What's the number?"

She punched a number in for the security code. When the buzzer released, he pulled open the door and motioned for her to go in. He followed her straight to the elevators, where one waited for them. He walked in with her and pressed the third floor.

She smiled. "Are you always so observant?"

"Always."

And she believed him. She wished he was the kind of person she could call on to help her. But he was a good man, and she didn't want him to get hurt. "I can't tell you, you know."

"You will tell me."

She frowned at him. "No. I won't. I can't get you hurt too."

He rounded on her. "Who hurt you?"

She took a step back and shook her head. "Not me."

He studied her for a long moment while the elevator slowly continued to climb. "Did you see somebody hurt somebody else? Did you see a crime committed?"

She winced. "How did you come to that conclusion?"

"Don't stall. This is important and time-sensitive. Did you see a crime committed?"

When the elevator doors opened, they both stepped through and walked to her apartment door. She put her keys into the lock and pushed her door open. She stepped inside, and he came in behind her.

"Answer the question."

She took a deep breath and slowly nodded. Now that they were inside her apartment, and she wouldn't be overheard, she had fewer qualms about telling him. If he was so determined to push his nose into her business, well, maybe this would finally scare him off.

She took another deep breath. "I saw the mayor of Houston standing in an alleyway beside another man. They were talking to a third man. The man at the mayor's side took out a small black handgun, and he shot the third guy, in the chest. He dropped to the ground. Looked dead already to me. While the mayor just stood there, watching."

"This morning? You saw that happen this morning?

She nodded. "And they saw me. That's why I ran. I didn't expect to see anybody there. I was just cutting through the back way. But I saw them. I turned and ran right into you."

"That might've been the worst morning of your life," he said with a gentle smile, "but running into me will make a shady day a great deal better."

"That's very …" She closed her mouth, searching for a word.

He reached out, tilted her chin toward him. "No, it's not conceited or arrogant. It's the truth. Because I'll help you, whether you like it or not."

Chapter 2

B AILEY DIDN'T EVEN know what to make of that statement. It had been a long time since she'd had anybody to share her burdens with. This man wanted to take them on even when they weren't his own.

She shook her head. "I can't have anybody hurt on my account." She turned to close the door. "Thank you for bringing me home."

He nodded, his gaze searching her small space from where he stood.

"What are you looking for?" she asked curiously.

"Your security. Looking for weaknesses, for places your defenses could be weak."

She shrugged. "I'm on the third-floor, and the most anybody can do is get in the front door."

"Do you have a balcony?" He walked over to the double French doors and opened them. He stepped out on the three-foot-wide balcony and stared over the edge. Apparently satisfied, he nodded and came back in. "You sleep with the windows and doors closed and locked?"

She shook her head. "No. When it's hot out, I sleep with everything open."

"Well, for the next few days, you sleep with them closed and locked, okay?"

"It won't make any difference. If an intruder is determined to get in, he will get in."

"Absolutely true," he said in surprise approval. "I'm glad you realize that. Because this isn't the safest place you could stay."

"No, but it's my space. And that matters a lot to me."

He gave her a nod, did a quick walk-through to make sure the place was okay.

She motioned toward the master bedroom. "Be my guest." She didn't mind him doing this at all. Besides, she would do it herself before she slept tonight. If sleep was possible. "Should I tell the police?"

He came out of her master bedroom and smiled. "Absolutely. My problem with that is, do you know anybody you can trust?"

She sucked in her breath with her arms over her chest. "Are you thinking the police won't help me?"

"If it was the mayor, then he will have people in place, in positions below him, keeping this quiet."

She grimaced. "In other words, some bad cops could be involved."

"There *could* be," he emphasized. "There are very few dirty cops in the world, at least in North America. The problem is, sometimes they get brought into a project without understanding all the ramifications or the different avenues interlocked in the project—avenues on the shady side. Some will believe you are lying to discredit the mayor."

"But why would I do that?"

"The police see stuff like this all the time. You wouldn't be the first, and you won't be the last. Just tell the police what you saw. First you should write everything down exactly as you saw it, with as much detail as you can remember, so you have something to refer to. The police will ask you about every detail. And you want to be clear."

"That makes sense."

She walked into the kitchen, opened a drawer and pulled out a small notepad. She took it over to the kitchen table and sat down. She should've thought to do this earlier. Not that she'd had time. Besides, shock was a devious thing. And it really destroyed her ability to function in any calm, reasonable way.

It took a bit to focus, but, when she eventually did, she carefully wrote down everything, from what she saw to describing the clothes the men wore, the sound of the bullets. She didn't have any details on the man who had been shot. She'd seen his face and that he wore dark clothing. She'd presumed it was a business transaction gone wrong between the three of them.

"And when you ran away, did they shout at you? Did they tell you to stop? Did you hear them get into a vehicle? All those little details are important."

She lifted her gaze to him but wasn't seeing his features, only the nightmare she'd tripped into. "I do remember the one man grabbing the mayor's arm and saying, 'Step back out of the way.'"

Dakota stepped closer to her. "Did you hear anything other than that? Did you feel anything? A jolt to your body, a burn, a sense of pressure, anything?"

She stared at him, feeling his confusion and angst pouring over her. "Not really. I almost fell, twisted my knee a bit. There was a weird sound, but it all blends into the nightmare." She frowned and put down her pen to rub her temple. "My headache is back. I can't tell you how ugly it is," she joked. "Feels like a major renovation is going on inside my brain."

He shook his head. "I'm so sorry. I let my guard down. I'm still shocked I actually hit you." He walked toward her and said abruptly, "Stand up, please."

"I had the headache … before, I think."

He motioned to her to stand up.

She did, then twisted slightly to look at him. "Why?"

Even just that movement made her head pound. She gasped and reached for her temple. "Damn that hurts."

"Take off your coat."

She raised her gaze to him and again asked, "Why?"

He stepped behind her and gently helped her drop the coat from her shoulders. As soon as it was off, she heard his gasp.

In a hard voice, he demanded, "I need to lift your shirt."

She turned and reached for the table as support when the room spun. "No."

"I won't hurt you," he said quietly. "I need to see why blood is all over your back."

She stared up at him in shock. "There's what?" She twisted, trying to see her back, only to shudder as waves of pain washed over her. "It can't be," she whispered. "No way I wouldn't know."

"Sometimes it takes a while."

She snorted. "There's no way. Not without actual blood showing."

He pulled up a chair and had her sit down on it backward.

When she leaned over the back of the chair, he checked out her back. "The blood soaked through your sweater and has partially dried. I'll get a dishcloth to soak the material again so I can lift it up without much pain to you and see just how badly hurt you are."

She protested, but he wasn't listening. He opened one of the drawers she pointed out, turned on the tap and ran warm water over the dishcloth. He came back and gently pressed it against her lower back. Instantly she cried out.

He did it several times, his face grim, until he placed the dishcloth, now very bloody, beside her. "Now I'll lift it up."

She could feel him gently peeling the material off her back. He tugged and pulled but it wasn't as painful as it could've been.

"Okay. Now you need to grab your coat and come with me."

She shook her head. "I'm too damn tired to go anywhere. It's nothing. Now that you've washed my back, it will be fine. I want to stay here and go to bed. I just need to rest."

He stepped around in front of her and crouched down so they were at eye level. "What you need are stitches. That wound is from a bullet that cut into the flesh. It needs to be cleaned, and you need stitches to close it."

She stared at him in shock. "How is that possible?"

He shrugged. "I'm thinking the man with the mayor turned to shoot you as you ran away." His voice hardened as he added, "And you're damn lucky. The bullet could have caused a lot more damage."

And then her back burned like fire. She pinched the bridge of her nose, feeling nausea working through her. "This is so stupid. I made it home with no pain. Sure I was tired and sore, but I figured it was from the stress. At the time I stumbled and almost fell before racing away. I just figured it was nothing."

"Well, that stumble saved your life," he said. He gently nudged her upright and draped the coat around her shoulders. "Let's go take care of this."

He led her out the door, making sure she had her purse, report tucked inside, and then used her keys to lock the door behind them.

She shook her head. "I still don't believe it."

"When you see the doctor, and he puts in stitches, I'm sure you'll believe it then."

DAKOTA HELPED HER into the SUV and drove her down the winding back roads toward the main street and headed to the closest hospital. He wasn't sure a twenty-four-hour clinic could handle a bullet wound. He also knew this would look exactly like what it was, and he didn't know if they would have to let the police know. Given the circumstances, he figured a hospital report of a gunshot wound was probably a good thing. It would give some credence to her story.

He pulled up beside the emergency entrance and walked around to help her out. She was still protesting. He smiled at her, tucked her arm through his and walked her toward the door.

"You can protest all you want, but there's no getting out of this." He cracked his lips at her. "I only nudged you with the vehicle but, to think that you were already shot and bleeding when I did it, just makes me feel all that much worse."

"Don't," she said, her voice getting fainter.

He watched her, seeing the color wash out of her skin as they got closer to the hospital door. "Are you going to faint on me?" he asked sharply. "I can pick you up and carry you, but I don't think it's the best thing for your back."

She shook her head and, in a grim voice, said, "I'll be fine."

Only she wasn't. Then he remembered the memories of her loss, and how many times she must have gone to the hospital to see her dying husband. This hospital visit would trigger so many of those memories. Still, she was stalwart as she moved forward. And he had to respect that. Hell, he had to respect her. She'd shown herself to be nothing but admirable thus far.

"How long?" he asked the triage nurse.

The woman gave him a harried look. "We have to treat those with more serious injuries first."

He nodded. "She's bleeding, and she'll pass out on us very soon."

She glanced over at Bailey and nodded. "I'll get her to see a doctor in the next few minutes."

He returned to Bailey's side and waited. Sure enough, about ten minutes later the nurse called Bailey over. She was led into one of the small treatment rooms. The white curtains closed around them. He sat at the side of the bed and waited for a doctor. Dakota wouldn't leave her side until he was pushed out.

They had to wait another ten to fifteen minutes before another nurse looked at the injury, frowned and disappeared.

A doctor came to see Bailey within minutes. He was efficient but casual as he studied the wound. "Do we need to call the police?"

Dakota nodded. "It would probably be a good idea."

The doctor stared at him. "Are you her husband?"

He shook his head. "A friend."

Understanding, the doctor said, "You need to wait outside while we treat her wound."

Bailey reached out and grasped Dakota's hand. "Can't he stay with me?"

"It can get a little busy and crowded in here," the doctor said gently. "As soon as we get you cleaned and stitched up, he can come back in for a few moments."

She nodded and let go of Dakota's hand. He stepped out and carried on right out to the front door. It was well past time to call Levi. Dakota should be home from his errands by now. Instead of being early, he wasn't sure he would make it back today at all.

Ice picked up the phone. Dakota quickly explained.

"What? The mayor?"

He heard the shock in her voice. She'd never been a big fan of politicians and had no patience for any of the double-dealings going on in their world, but, at the same time, Ice was a trooper. And she'd bend over backward to help anybody who needed it.

"What have you still got to do on your list?"

"Hang on." He pulled his list from his pocket and read over the four items left. "I'm not sure she's in any shape to go home. I can pick up the rest and make it back if need be."

"I can send somebody else in, but we're a little short-staffed now." She was distracted. "But I can also grab one of the other vehicles and come transfer the gear over."

"Wait until I hear what the doctor has to say. If she's okay and can stay overnight at the hospital, which I doubt, I could run home. Otherwise she'll need somebody to take her back to her place, and I'm not comfortable leaving her all alone."

"Does she have any friends and family to look after her for the night?"

He explained about her husband.

Ice was sympathetic. "There's an easy answer. I have a medical clinic, which is almost always empty. Bring her here, and we'll get her settled onto a bed, and, if we need to do anything for her, then we can look after her here."

Dakota smiled. "Ice, you have a soft heart."

"Don't you tell anybody else that," she warned. "Keep me informed. If you get a chance to pick up the rest of the stuff, great. If not, we'll make a second trip tomorrow."

"Will do." He put away his phone and walked back into the emergency waiting area. With the nurses coming and going, he finally stopped one to ask, "Is she likely to stay overnight?"

The nurse shook her head. "I don't think so. The doctors aren't done in there yet. It's clean, but it's deep. She'll need to rest and not move for the next few days. We can't have her ripping the stitches open."

He nodded. "I have a place where she can stay."

The nurse shot him a bright smile. "Good. She'll need looking after."

Dakota nodded. At the same time, he realized he forgot to ask Ice about any cops here who they could count on. He hadn't been in town long enough to know who were their allies and who weren't. But Ice would know. She'd spent the last couple years cultivating goodwill among all their neighbors. They would have a certain number of police they counted on.

His phone rang just then. He walked back out the front door and answered it. "Hello?"

"This is Detective Mannford. I just got off the phone with Ice. She told me a pretty far-fetched story."

"I heard the same story. Bailey has a bullet wound across her back in confirmation as well. I have her account written down of what she saw."

"You have that in your hands?"

"No, it's in her purse. She's currently being treated in emergency, so you can't speak with her just yet."

"Do you believe her?"

"I believe that the woman I found was in shock and dealing with some major trauma. I got her hot coffee and a meal. Then I took her home. That whole time she wasn't quite there. She was still dealing with a shock reaction. It was only as I got her home and heard her story that I realized something much more serious could be going on. I took off her coat, and that's when I saw her back was covered in blood."

"Damn. The mayor?"

"Yes, that's who she said it was."

"Did she have reason to know exactly who the mayor is? Enough to recognize him from a distance?"

"He's been extremely visible lately, so it's certainly within reason that she would. Also his face is on a lot of the billboards around town, and he's been lobbying for his latest bill to pass. Not to mention, with the re-election coming up, his campaign posters are everywhere."

"Yeah. Did she give a description of the other man?"

"All she remembers is he was taller than the mayor, and all three men were dressed in suits. She did see him pull the trigger and saw the third man collapse."

"We don't have a dead body. I need the location of where she saw this happen. There's got to be a blood trail or forensic proof of some nature there."

"I don't have a street name." Dakota stared at the blue sky. "You have to wait, like I said, and talk to her. I know the general area because I saw her running, but I don't know exactly which alleyway it happened in."

"Okay, how long do you think she'll be?"

"Probably an hour. The doctor is working on her right now. I don't know if they are shooting her up with painkillers, and I don't know what shape she'll be in, so you're likely better off if you're here as soon as possible, just in case."

"Or I could catch you tomorrow at her apartment …"

"I'm taking her back to the compound. Ice can keep an eye on her there."

"She lives alone?" the detective asked in a sharp voice.

"Not only alone, she's a widow, still dealing with the grief of losing her husband eighteen months ago."

"Friends? Family?"

"Not that I know of."

"That makes her easy to get rid of, as not too many people would kick up a fuss. But they'd have to find her first." His voice turned thoughtful. "The mayor has a lot of resources, including access to the traffic cams if he wanted to track her movements. So it wouldn't be hard to find out where she lived."

"Exactly. She does work, but I'm not sure where."

"Well, let's get her full name for a start."

Dakota gave her full name and her home address. "We had coffee at a little tiny diner around the corner. I think it's called Nexus Café."

"I know the area. Which direction was she coming from when she ran into the street?"

He explained and added, "My take is it happened fairly quickly. She wasn't super soaked at the time, though it was raining hard."

"Okay. I'll drive around through a couple of those blocks and see if I find anything, then I'll come to the hospital."

Feeling better, Dakota pocketed his phone and headed

back in. He sat down in the waiting room and sent Saul a quick text, explaining what had happened. Saul was up north, probably wouldn't get the message immediately. But he liked to be kept in the loop.

Eventually the doctor came back out and walked over to Dakota. "I still have some paperwork to do."

"Detective Mannford is on his way," Dakota said. "He'll be on point with this one."

The doctor looked happy. "Glad to hear that. It could've been much worse. Even if that angle had just been slightly different, she would be dead right now."

His face grim, Dakota nodded. "I was afraid of that. She sat all through lunch without any sign of pain. It was only after I got her home and I started asking questions about exactly what had happened that I realized there could be so much more to this."

"Shock is a powerful thing. She wouldn't have been aware until it started to wear off. Then the pain would have hit, and she'd have been in agony."

"She started complaining about a bad headache."

The doctor nodded. "That happens too sometimes." He pulled out his pen and paper. "I presume you will be looking after her?"

Dakota nodded.

The doctor wrote a prescription for painkillers and another for antibiotics. He handed them to Dakota. "Both are necessary. That shot went deep. She's to see her doctor in seven to ten days to get the stitches removed." And with that he turned and walked away.

Dakota pocketed both prescriptions. As he crossed to head where Bailey was, a man strode in. The look on his face, his back and shoulders straight, all said *cop* to Dakota.

He stepped in front of him and asked, "Detective Mannford?"

The detective nodded and held out his hand.

"Dakota Languor." The two men shook hands. "I told the doctor you would be point on this case. He said he's still got to write up a report and file it."

Detective Mannford said, "No problem. We'll take care of it." He looked around. "Where is she?"

"I'm right here," Bailey said in a weak voice.

Dakota turned to see Bailey, standing on her own two feet but looking ready to collapse at any moment. He raced over and gently placed an arm around her. "Easy."

She gave him a lopsided smile. "The nurse did say they'd give me a wheelchair, but I refused. I can walk, but I'm not so sure about sitting."

She nodded to the detective but dropped her gaze to the floor.

Dakota leaned forward and whispered, "He's clear."

She gave him a shuttered look and nodded. But he realized just his word wouldn't make her believe it. And that was the way it should be. She had to make her own decisions as to what she believed for her own safety.

The detective looked at her closely. "Can you answer a few questions for me? I've already heard a general accounting from Dakota."

"If it's fast," she said. "I want to go home and lie down."

Dakota stayed quiet. This wasn't the time to tell her that she wasn't going home.

"I need the location where the shooting occurred."

She closed her eyes and described where she was and what she'd seen. Dakota watched as the detective wrote it down.

Finally he put away his notepad. "I'll contact you tomorrow to see if you can remember anything else."

She smiled and nodded.

Dakota took that cue and led her gently out the front door back to his SUV. "We need to get your prescriptions filled."

"There's a little drugstore around the corner from my place that I have an account with," she said.

He nodded. When she was safely buckled in, her back stiffened as she leaned forward. *It must hurt,* he thought. He carefully drove back to where she lived and her local drugstore. "I need to go inside too. They don't just give the prescriptions to anybody."

"If you think you can." He helped her from the vehicle and led her slowly into the pharmacy.

When they made it to the counter, the woman looked up and smiled. "Bailey, obviously you haven't had a good day."

She shook her head gently. "Nope, but I'll be fine." She paid for the prescriptions, and he took her back to the SUV. She whispered, "Thank you for doing this. All I want to do now is go to bed."

He handed her a bottled water and pointed at her pills. After she took one of each, he explained. "Well, unfortunately I have bad news for you. You're not going home. I'm taking you back to where I live, in the compound with several highly trained medical personnel who will look after you tonight."

She stared at him and shook her head. "Please, no. I don't want strangers in my world right now."

"I know that. But you've been alone for a long time. You can't be alone right now. Unfortunately I also have to make a few stops before I can leave town."

She groaned and settled against the seat. He reached over her and pressed a couple of the seat buttons so she could recline more. She settled in, crying out slightly, and then didn't say another word.

He quickly drove to his next three stops. Each time she barely even moved. When he hit the last one, loaded up the rest of the groceries, he called Ice. "I'm done. I have her. We're on the way home."

"Good. We have a room ready for her."

Chapter 3

BAILEY WOKE UP as the gentle rolling motion came to an even gentler stop. Dakota took his foot off the accelerator and let the vehicle roll forward. She tried to sit up, crying out in pain. She gasped and collapsed back down again. There she lay, taking several deep breaths.

"Take it easy. We're at my place."

"I don't even know you," she whispered. "You don't know me. Why are you taking care of me?"

In the dark recesses of her mind was the concept that maybe he was out for something that wasn't in her best interests, but the thought was briefly considered and then tossed away. Of all things, she knew this man wasn't a rapist or serial killer. He'd done nothing but try to look after her.

Letting her eyes open enough to adjust to the darkness around her, she waited as Dakota came around the vehicle and opened her door. Gentle hands unhooked her seat belt. With his help, she swung her legs around and slid to the ground. Just putting her weight on her heels sent shock waves up her spine, and pain rippled through her system. "I think I could use another painkiller now."

"We'll get you one really quick," he said.

She heard multiple voices as doors opened, and a stream of men and women exited the building. Bailey looked up at what appeared to be a massive cement structure. "Is this your home? This doesn't look like a house. It looks like … a compound." She stared at the six feet … seven feet … maybe even eight feet of wire fencing surrounding the property. "It's fenced."

"It needs to be," he said cheerfully. "And no worries. It is a house. … At least part of it is." He tossed his keys to somebody. "Levi, the back is full. I did manage to get everything on the list."

Levi walked around, hitting buttons to unlock the vehicle as people unloaded it. Levi stepped in front of Bailey, his gaze assessing, careful.

She offered him a smile. "I did try to argue with Dakota about not bringing me here."

"He was right to bring you here," the man said gently. "I'm Levi."

A stunning woman stepped up beside him. "And I'm Ice. Let's get you inside where you can lie down."

Just the thought of lying down and being out of this agony brought tears to her eyes. With Dakota's help, she stepped away from the vehicle and slowly made her way to the door, while the crowd loaded with boxes and bags from the SUV disappeared. Inside, she realized they were on the main floor of an incredibly large house. Beautiful stone floors and what appeared to be stone walls greeted her. On the left was a massive dining room with a table that seemed to go on forever.

"I can't imagine what size kitchen and how much staff you must have to accommodate this place," she muttered.

Ice reached out and gently caressed her other arm. "Thankfully the place runs itself very well."

They stopped in front of an elevator. Bailey stared at Ice. "Something seems very wrong about an elevator inside the house."

"But, in this case, it's a good thing," Dakota said cheer-fully. "It saves us from helping you up and down the stairs."

She winced. "Good point." She knew her energy was fading, but she didn't realize just how quickly. She was desperate to lie down. The elevator opened. "It's almost like the inside of a castle."

She hadn't realized she'd spoken out loud until Ice said, "Not quite a castle. But a huge mansion, yes."

After the elevator ride, they went down small hallways until Ice stepped in front of them and opened a door. She looked at Dakota and said, "Let's settle her in."

Bailey stepped inside to see one of the most elegant and yet casually comfortable bedrooms she'd ever seen before. Her gaze landed on the bed, and she moaned. "I sure hope I get to lie down on that now."

Ice walked over and flipped back the covers. "Absolutely. I understand from Dakota he didn't get a chance to return to your apartment and get you some clothes, so we have just something simple here for you to sleep in for the night. I have towels for you here too. First things first—let's get you into bed so you can rest."

Dakota gave her hand a squeeze. "Let me grab the pre-scriptions while Ice helps you into bed." And she watched as he walked out the room, feeling a sense of loss.

Ice patted her hand gently. "Come on. Let's get you into bed."

With Ice's help, she stripped down to her underwear, then slipped on the huge man's T-shirt that fell to her knees but was soft against her wound, then eased onto the bed. With Ice holding the blankets up, Bailey slowly collapsed sideways against the pillow and tucked her legs underneath.

She moaned as soon as her head hit the soft pillow and whispered, "Thank you. I'm so grateful to be in this bed right now."

"It will get better. But tomorrow won't be easy."

"Right. Things are always worse on the second day," Bailey whispered, her eyes falling closed.

"They are, indeed. I think I hear Dakota coming." Ice walked to the door and out into the hall.

Bailey could hear Ice's footsteps as she made her way up the hallway toward the stairs. Then she heard hushed voices.

Dakota walked in the bedroom. "Don't fall asleep yet. You have to take your pills."

Just the thought of sitting back up again was enough to make her cry. But she'd made it this far and, dammit, she'd make it through the rest. She propped herself slowly on her elbows, and, with his help, she took the pills as if she were a child and swallowed them obediently. She handed the glass back to him and whispered, "Thank you."

She collapsed again and let her eyes drift closed.

"Now sleep. I'll check on you in an hour or so to see how you're doing."

She nodded her head, although the movement was probably barely noticeable for the lack of effort she put into it. She could already feel sleep reaching out for her. And she was so damn grateful to reach back. The last thing she heard as she drifted off was Dakota saying to Ice, "I'll stand watch."

It confused her, because she didn't understand why anyone would stand watch. But then she didn't give a damn, and she fell asleep anyway.

BACK DOWNSTAIRS WAS organized chaos as the SUV was

emptied of its heavy load. Several of the women were in the kitchen helping Alfred put away the massive grocery order that Dakota had brought back. This wasn't even the meat or the fresh vegetables. This was just stock items for the pantry.

Dakota walked through the dining room to the coffee-pot and poured himself a cup. He leaned against the sideboard for a few moments. He shouldn't stay. He needed to go back to her side.

"She'll be fine for a little while," Ice said.

"The SUV's unloaded," Levi said. "Let's sit down, and you can tell us exactly what happened."

Dakota pulled out a chair and sat down at the table, holding his coffee mug in his hand. "I don't know most of it. I'll tell what I do know." He started with the heavy rain and her running in front of him on the road. "Of course I got out and raced to see what had happened. She stood there for a moment, talking to me normally, and then she just bolted. I ran after her." He continued right through to the hospital visit, talking to the doctor and then Detective Mannford showing up. "So, I brought her here as per instructions." He glanced over at Ice and smiled. "Thanks, by the way. I wasn't exactly sure what to do with her."

"She's welcome to stay for a couple days until she's capable of looking after herself again," Ice said firmly. "You can grab some clothes from her apartment later."

Dakota nodded. "That's no problem. I'll get a list from her of what she'd like to have picked up."

"In the meantime, Detective Mannford will follow-up with the hospital reports and the information she gave him."

"I feel like I should call him. He left the hospital the same time we did. So he certainly should have had time to get to the alleyway and check it out."

"With the heavy rain, most of the evidence would have been washed away."

He slumped in his chair. "I should've thought of that. It just never connected in my mind. I was hoping a pool of blood would be somewhere along the line that would give some forensic evidence to back up her story."

"Do you doubt her story?" Ice asked.

He shook his head. "I don't doubt she believes it's the truth. As to if it is the truth, I don't know. I didn't see what she saw. I didn't hear what she heard. And I certainly didn't pay the penalty for being in the wrong place at the wrong time."

Alfred walked in just then. "Everybody's already eaten. Can I get you a plate?"

Dakota stared at him and then nodded. "Thank you, Alfred. That would be much appreciated."

Alfred disappeared into the kitchen as various members of the compound family gathered around the dining table, interested in the new arrival.

"We've all heard a variation of the story, but we're still lacking details," Sienna said.

Dakota snorted. "Well, we all are. It looks like she saw a murder and was shot while fleeing, only didn't realize what had happened until later."

"It's an odd angle for her to get shot while fleeing," Merk said.

Dakota nodded. "She stumbled and nearly collapsed, wrenched her knee from that. So I figure that's when the bullet scraped along her spine."

Merk whistled. "If she'd been upright, she would've been a goner."

"Exactly. She wasn't intended to survive."

"Are we expecting trouble here then?" Sienna asked.

No fear or concern was evident in her voice. But then she'd been here longer than Dakota and had settled in nicely. He'd heard the story of her arrival too, and he knew she would understand Bailey's need for a haven.

"I don't know," he said. "Someone would have to know that she was with me. Somebody would have to know who I was. And they'd have to find my vehicle, track the license plate, or follow us home." He picked up his coffee and thought about everything that had gone on. "It's not that it would be hard to track the vehicle, yet I don't *think* anybody followed us."

Levi nodded. "Still, we aren't taking any chances. The compound goes on lockdown until further notice."

Dakota glanced around at all the faces of people who had become so very near and dear to him so quickly. "I really appreciate you guys helping her out."

"There's no way we wouldn't help. This is what we do," Levi said. "I'm not sure it is what we set out to do, but helping people is what we do."

Ice reached over and tucked her hand inside Levi's.

Dakota watched and smiled. He wanted that. He wanted to know he had the same mind-set as another person, somebody who understood him inside and out, that words weren't necessary to know they agreed with your every thought. He didn't need a doormat; he didn't want a yes-person. He wanted somebody who would argue and talk things over with him, but, at the same time, when it came to full values and core issues, there would be no arguments because they'd both be on the same side of an issue. So many people here had found just that.

Before he'd arrived, he had been teased about Legendary

Security, the brunt of a joke about some matchmaking going on. But living with all these couples was such a weird feeling. Levi and Ice didn't just have a business here; they had a family, and it was something Dakota had never expected to be a part of. But now that he was, he didn't want to do anything to jeopardize it.

"Is it okay for me to stay here for a couple days?" he asked Levi. "Or am I scheduled to go out on a job?"

Levi shook his head. "Your job is to look after Bailey. Until we get to the end of this and find out what our illustrious mayor is up to," he said with a sarcastic tone, "then that's where you belong."

Chapter 4

BAILEY OPENED HER eyes, feeling overheated, forcing her to push back the blankets. Only to cry out. Every movement hurt. As she rolled over, her back pain flared up again. The painkillers had helped, and she sure hoped the antibiotics would take care of any other problems. The last thing she wanted was an infection and a fever from the injury.

Of course, if she'd known she would get shot, she would've changed her outfit. On that slightly humorous note, she tried to sit up, using the headboard to keep her back rigid. Finally she made it, gasping with pain. She sat there and looked around the room, pleased to see it had the air of a home not a hotel. A bathroom was right in front of her. The only problem was getting to it.

Considering how weak she was, she used the headboard to pull herself upright, and then, using the wall for support, she slowly made her way across to the bathroom.

After using the facilities, she winced at her reflection in the mirror. Her hair was a nightmare. She quickly tried to straighten it. She looked tired, but she couldn't do much about that.

She wasn't sure if she should stay here or go downstairs, not knowing the house rules. She didn't mind staying in her room, but it was hardly polite.

Determined to not make anyone regret helping her out, she slowly reached for a bathrobe and placed it around her shoulders. She took a deep breath, waiting for the pain. At the very least, maybe she could say hi and then come back. She opened the door and stepped out into the hallway.

She didn't have her purse or her cell phone, so she had no idea what time it was. She turned the corner and headed down a wider hallway. She marveled at the architecture reflected in this huge space—a whole lot of medieval castle elements. Seeing the elevator, she smiled. "I remember those." She stepped inside and read the numbers.

She pushed the button for the ground floor and waited for it to take her downstairs. When the door opened again, she wasn't sure where to go, but a lot of noise came from the right. She slowly made her way toward the commotion, taking another right, and ended up in a massive kitchen.

An older man prepped a single plate of food. He looked up; surprise crossed his face. Immediately he rushed over to her. "Are you sure you should be up?"

She reached out and grasped his hand. "I feel much better. I think it must be the painkillers," she admitted.

He smiled, hooked her arm through his and said gently, "My name is Alfred. Come on. I'll take you in to Dakota."

He walked her slowly into the noisy dining room. She didn't recognize anybody.

Alfred cleared his throat, and there was silence. Everyone turned to look her way. She retreated, but Alfred patted her hand. "Don't you worry. You'll fit right in, my dear. Everyone, this is Bailey. She's awake and on her feet, even though she shouldn't be."

Dakota bounded up from the far side of the table and strode toward her. Relief washed through her at the sight of him. "There you are," she cried.

He wrapped an arm carefully around her shoulders for support. "I thought you'd be asleep for hours yet."

She smiled. "As much as I'd like to be back asleep, I'm awake. I wasn't sure if I should stay in my room or come find you," she confessed.

"You didn't have to worry on that score. I'd planned to come check on you in a little bit."

Ice stood, and her gaze traveled over Bailey, making a head-to-toe assessment of her condition.

Bailey smiled. "You have medical training by any chance?"

"Field variety but yes."

Dakota slowly walked her around the dining table to an empty seat beside him.

"This has got to be the largest table I've ever seen in my life."

"That's because it's four put together," Levi said.

Bailey recognized a few of the faces now, but the others were all a blur from when Dakota had brought her here. "I'm sorry. I don't remember most of you."

Dakota pulled out the chair and helped her sit down. "How could you," he joked. "They weren't all here when you arrived."

Seated, her back felt better. She smiled up at him with thanks and glanced around the table full of strange faces. "Thank you for the haven. My name is Bailey Hoskins," she said more formally.

Dakota did the introductions, but the names came fast, and she knew she'd never remember them all. "It will take me a while to remember everyone," she admitted.

"Don't rush it," a woman on the far side said. "By the

time you figure it out, the rest of our team will be back, and you'll be confused again. This is only half of us right now."

Bailey knew her surprise showed on her face when the others chuckled. "Wow." She turned to look at Dakota. "You said you worked for a security company?"

He nodded and pointed toward Ice and Levi. "It's their company."

Bailey looked over at the twosome and smiled. "So, it's you I have to thank for the assistance."

Ice said firmly, "No thanks required. It's important you get back on your feet again."

"Of course I really would like to know if you're sure that the mayor was involved in the shooting," Levi said, leaning forward. "He's not my favorite person, so I won't be too upset if he was."

She winced. "It was him. I saw his face clearly."

Levi studied her for a long moment, then nodded. "Good enough for me." He turned to Ice. "Another regime will fall."

Ice chuckled. "This is just a mini-regime."

"I almost miss that. Toppling governments is a lot of work but fun."

Bailey listened to the banter back and forth, but she wasn't sure if they were joking or if they were serious. She figured it was a little bit of both.

Alfred arrived with a plate of food for Dakota. As soon as he set it down, he turned to Bailey. "May I get you a plate of the same?"

She glanced over at the roast beef and gravy and vegetables and could feel her mouth water. "Yes, please, if you have it to spare."

Dakota chuckled. "If there's one thing Alfred likes to do,

it's feed people. So it's okay if he makes something fresh for you."

She leaned over as Alfred walked away and whispered, "You're lucky to have him."

Dakota leaned back and said, "And we know it."

She smiled. "Any word from Detective Mannford?"

Ice shook her head. "Not yet but I should give him a quick call anyway." She hopped to her feet and disappeared around the corner. Her movements were fast, exact and efficient.

And it surprised Bailey. "I didn't mean she had to call now."

Levi shook his head. "Always better to do what you can do now, instead of putting it off."

Alfred came back a few moments later. As he set the food in front of her, Ice returned. "Detective Mannford said no visible signs or evidence was left where you described it happening. He found no sign of a body or a large pool of blood at this point."

"Of course there isn't." She frowned, hating for anyone to think she'd made this up. Why had she expected anything to be easy? She'd just assumed forensic evidence would be left behind, like in the television shows. "I guess he didn't find any gun casings?"

"He said it was too dark to tell more than that, but he'll return in the morning. He's hoping the puddles will have dried up enough that they can search for casings or other evidence left behind. He wants to go back before the killer thinks to double-check for evidence himself."

Bailey nodded. She cut into the roast beef, lifted a bite, and almost moaned in joy. "Oh, wow. I hope you pay Alfred lots. He's worth every penny."

Levi grinned and admitted, "We would be lost without him."

Dakota kept a close eye on her and could tell she tried not to let him see her discomfort, but occasionally she'd shift positions, and he'd catch the pain whisper across her face. After she'd been sitting here for a full hour, fatigue pulled at her. Nothing like a warm stomach to make her want to fall back asleep again.

Dakota leaned closer and whispered, "Are you ready to go back to bed?"

She gave him a lopsided smile. "I think I'm ready to fall asleep again."

"I'll take her up to her room now," Dakota announced, standing up. "Your purse is here on the sideboard too. We'll take it up with us."

Giving her his arm, he waited for her to stand. He knew her back had to be killing her, but the painkiller should be helping. He glanced over at Ice. "She needs her bandage checked."

Ice hopped up. "Let's take her to the medical clinic first. We'll change the bandage so she can go right to bed."

"Medical clinic?"

Moving slowly at Dakota's side, she used his arm to walk, her back throbbing with every step.

"We have a full-on medical clinic here. Ice's a medic, but her father is a doctor. He owns a private hospital in California. She's done a lot of different training, although she's not a licensed nurse."

Bailey shook her head. "Wow, I sure hit the right vehicle."

"I think I hit you," he corrected. "Not the other way around. I'm still having nightmare flashbacks about that."

She squeezed his arm. "No point. I have enough for both of us."

He shot her a look to see if she was serious, realizing of course she was. She'd seen a man murdered, then ran for her life, got hit by a vehicle, only to find out when it was all over she'd been burned by a bullet. She'd have nightmares for the rest of her life.

In the medical clinic, they stopped so Bailey could stop and stare. Slowly she spun in a circle. "Oh, my goodness, this is just like a hospital."

Ice turned and beamed at Bailey.

Dakota smiled. He hadn't realized just how proud of the space Ice really was, but it was evident in every line of her body.

"It took a lot of time and effort to make this the way we wanted it," she explained. "The first couple months we were here, we actually had a doctor with us, to help get it right. Unfortunately this medical clinic has been christened several times."

"Did anybody die here?" Bailey asked quietly.

"None of our men did. Mexican guerrillas came after several of us on the compound. They weren't so lucky." She walked to the first bed. "Hop up here."

"Good." Bailey stumbled over to the bed Ice patted with her hand.

"Take off your bathrobe, give it to Dakota, and then we'll just take care of your back."

Dakota stood in front of Bailey, so she could see him, but also so she wouldn't feel exposed when Ice checked her wound.

She handed over the bathrobe and struggled until she lay on the clean bed. With her hands at her side, Ice gently lifted her huge hand-me-down T-shirt that served as a nightgown until it exposed the center of her back. She used a blanket to cover her legs and hips.

In an efficient move, Ice removed the bandage. "That's quite a burn mark."

Bailey lifted her head and frowned. "Burn?"

"It's what we call it when the bullet scrapes through the edge of the skin and burns into the tissue," Ice explained. "It's really just a superficial wound when compared to what the bullet could have done."

As she lay here, Ice's gentle ministrations were cooling and soothing. Ice carefully cleaned the wound, put a new bandage over it, taping it in place. Then she pulled down Bailey's makeshift nightgown. "There, you're all done."

Bailey slowly shifted so she sat up again. She smiled at Ice. "I hardly felt a thing."

Ice chuckled. "Well, I took it easy on you. But the rest of these guys, I'm pretty rough with."

Dakota rolled his eyes. "Ice is a softy on the inside."

Bailey gently slipped off the edge of the bed to the floor. "How long is the wound?"

"About four inches. I didn't count the stitches, but quite a few are in there."

"In other words, a big scar?"

Ice shrugged. "It'll be a scar for sure. Doesn't have to be a very big one. Depends on how well you heal. Around this place, scars are just war wounds. We all have them—way more than we want to show anyone—and they all come with bad memories. Now you have one of your own."

On that note, she patted Dakota on the shoulder and said, "Make sure she gets to bed safely." Then she turned and walked out.

With Dakota guiding her, Bailey made her way to the elevator and upstairs to the second floor. "This place is incredible."

Dakota smiled. "It's pretty crazy. I haven't been here very long myself. But at least I know my way around now. Yet that was still the first time I've had to go to the medical clinic."

"Good to know you weren't injured enough to need medical care."

He nodded quietly. "She meant what she said about somebody attacking the compound. It's happened several times."

She shook her head. "It's hard to imagine. But, of all the places I could end up, this is likely one of the best."

"Which is exactly why I brought you here. Ice and Levi also have great connections within the law enforcement world. Not just in Houston but across the country. Including the FBI and the Texas Rangers."

"Wow. Thank you so much for hitting me then." She shot him a comical look.

He gave a bark of laughter. "I never thought I'd hear that statement in my life."

They arrived outside her door. He stepped forward, opened it, turned on the lights and held the door so she could walk in.

She stared at the bed. "I have to go to the bathroom first. Then I'll be tucked in for the night." As she made her way to the bathroom, she turned to look at him. "I'll be fine now. You don't have to wait for me."

He crossed his arms, leaned against the open door, not saying a word.

She rolled her eyes. "I guess that means you'll wait?" She

shook her head without waiting to see or hear the answer and walked into the bathroom. She silently closed the door. She really wanted a shower, but she knew that wasn't feasible with the bandage on her back.

A brand-new toothbrush and a small tube of toothpaste waited for her. She smiled. Ice thought of everything.

Also a folded washcloth was off to the side. She used the facilities and washed her hands and face and brushed her teeth. When she was done, she opened the door and made her way to the bed.

She hadn't made the bed when she'd walked out earlier, but, while she'd been in the bathroom, Dakota must have straightened the bedding and then turned back the covers so she could get in easier. She stood beside the bed and dropped the bathrobe from her shoulders. She should have handed it to him, but it was too late. He stepped up and held her arm. She slowly lowered herself to the mattress.

When she was finally flattened out, he pulled the covers over her. Then he grabbed the bathrobe and hung it on a hook on the back of the door.

"You make a great babysitter," she whispered.

"No, I do not." He walked to the door.

"Good night," she called out. "And thanks for taking such great care of me."

"Good night." He hesitated at the doorway, turned, then asked, "You want the door open or closed?"

She thought about it for a moment and then whispered, "Closed please."

The last thing she heard was the gentle *click* as the door latch was engaged. She smiled. She had no idea how she got to be so lucky, but she was damned grateful. She closed her eyes and let sleep take over.

DAKOTA WALKED BACK downstairs. It'd been a hell of a long day in many ways. He was restless, rather desperate to discuss today's events with his friends. He found Ice and Levi still sitting at one of the smaller kitchen tables. They both looked up at him when he walked in.

"She's almost asleep now," he said. He turned and leaned against the counter and stared at them both. "Not sure I'll sleep tonight though."

Levi nodded. "Nightmares are something we're all well used to."

"Any update from Detective Mannford?"

Ice shook her head. "Not since I called. There won't be any new info until morning."

He nodded. "I'll do some research on the mayor and the people he has business dealings with. Maybe, if we can come up with some faces for her to look at tomorrow, it'll jog her memory."

"That's a good idea," Levi said. "And make sure you do some research on her too. I don't doubt that this happened to her today, but you don't know who she is fully yet."

Dakota nodded. "I'm pretty damn sure about what I do know. However, as we all are aware, information is power, so I'll do my due diligence there too."

"Does she have a vehicle?" Ice asked.

He shrugged. "I'm not sure if she does or not. She was running when I hit her, and she was only a few blocks from her apartment." He frowned at Ice. "Why?"

"I just wondered if it needed to be collected."

He was relieved she was thinking about it as he sure hadn't thought to ask. "Better it stays where it is, particularly if it's at her apartment. Keeping it under surveillance will burn their manpower and keep them guessing. I'll ask her about it later." He walked toward the doorway. "I'll head to my room, do a little online digging before I call it a night."

The two called out good-night as he left the kitchen. He detoured to the dishwasher, put his coffee cup in and went upstairs to his room, next to Bailey's. He didn't know if that was deliberate on Ice's part but figured it was. Not only would he hear Bailey if she called out, but he could keep an eye on her.

Once in his room, he took a quick shower, put on clean boxers and dropped onto the bed with his laptop. A few minutes later he was deep in research on the mayor. Being relatively new to the area, Dakota didn't know any of the names or issues.

An hour later he was certainly much better versed. And he wasn't impressed with what he had read about the mayor either.

According to the pictures he'd found, the mayor was often seen with two men. Whether they were bodyguards or aides, Dakota didn't know, but one was tall and had more of a bruiser look to him. Dakota tracked down several good images of both the mayor's face and his aides, saving them on his laptop. In the morning he'd ask Bailey if she recognized any of them.

Then he did research on Bailey herself. Searching for her last name and then her first name. One of the initial things that popped up was the obituary for her husband. He settled back to read it.

The story was as she had given him—just a brief description. The images of the grief-stricken widow hit him hard. She really had been through a lot lately. He looked for earlier photos of her and came up with a couple from social media.

Back then she was at least twenty pounds heavier than she was now and a whole lot happier. He put away his laptop and muttered, "You might've been happier, but you're a survivor now, and that's worth a lot today and into the future. We'll get you through this. Don't worry."

He turned out the lights and rolled over. With any luck, he'd get some decent sleep himself.

Chapter 5

BAILEY OPENED HER eyes, startled at the unfamiliar room. Awareness kicked in, and all the recent memories came flooding back, along with the pain. Her back throbbed, and an uncomfortable heat spread throughout her body. Obviously her painkillers had worn off. But she also needed to go to the bathroom. She rolled to her side before trying to stand. A whimper escaped—the sound extra loud in the dark room. She didn't know if anybody was close enough to hear her, but she didn't want to disturb them. She made her way to the bathroom.

When she was done, she grabbed a glass of water. Back at her bedside, she studied the night table and realized her painkillers weren't with her.

The last she'd seen them, Dakota had them in his hand. She glanced around, feeling just crappy enough that the tears waited to pour. "Damn. I don't need this."

She picked up her phone, but of course she didn't have his number. She couldn't text him to see if he was still awake, and she had no idea where in this mansion he could be. But the pain was getting so bad that she would find her way to the medical clinic if it meant somebody would give her more painkillers. She sat on the bed and tried to hold back her tears.

The pain intensified. She stood up and paced, walking

herself through it. Something that she and her husband had done many a time during his treatments. It would take his attention off the pain and let his body adapt.

She walked and walked in the spacious room. And her pain still wasn't any better. When a knock sounded on the door, she turned, startled, and cried out.

Instantly the door opened, and Dakota stepped in, frowned at her. "Why aren't you asleep?"

"The pain woke me," she admitted. "I would take more medicine, but I don't know where it is."

His gaze went to the night table and then back to her. "Damn. They're in my room." He shook his head and stepped out, calling over his shoulder, "I'll be right back."

She was so relieved. She went to the bed and sat down. He returned almost instantly with two bottles in his hand. He handed her one and then placed the second one on her night table. "Take the painkillers now. Those are the antibiotics on the night table. You took two last night, but it's too soon to take two more."

"How early is it?"

"It's almost five."

She nodded. "I slept longer than I expected then."

"And not as long as I'd hoped," he said with a smile.

She popped two of the painkillers into her mouth and downed them with a glass of water, then lay sideways on the bed.

"You will sleep some more?"

She shook her head. "I don't think so. I'm naturally an early riser, so that's probably it. On the other hand, the medication has quite a punch to it, so the painkillers may put me back under."

"Good enough. Let's give it a half hour and see if you

can fall asleep again." He walked over and sat down in the big easy chair beside the bed.

She looked at him. "You can go back to your own bed and go to sleep, you know."

"I know," he said, "but I'll stay here and wait."

She gave him a sweet smile. "While you're here, tell me about this place and what you do."

She tucked the pillow up under her head and listened as he explained about Levi inheriting the house and how he and Ice had come together and built up the property and the business.

"Wow, that's a labor of love for them." She was overwhelmed at the size of the operation they'd created.

"In many ways, yes. But then this place has become almost a matchmaking center," he said with a grin. "All those women downstairs, other than Ice, came as Levi added more new recruits. Each one of the women has a partner off on a job right now or here working at the compound."

She smiled. "You know? That's a sweet thought."

He chuckled. "I'm not sure how that works. But my buddy Saul, who came here with me, he's already found somebody."

"Maybe it's not this mansion. Maybe it's Texas in general."

"Maybe," he said. "I can't say I've been looking though."

"Neither have I," she admitted. "I'm not sure it works that way."

"No, but, in your case, you need to move on. It's hard, but that's the easiest way to get back into living your life."

She nodded, and she tried to keep talking, but her eyelids drooped. "I think I can sleep now," she whispered.

"Good. Go to sleep. I'll stay here for a few minutes to

make sure you're good."

She snuggled deeper into the blankets and whispered, "You're a very nice man."

"No," he said quietly. "I'm really not."

She struggled to answer but it took too much energy and decided against it. With each breath she let herself drift deeper into sleep. When she woke up the next time, she was all alone again; yet, as she assessed her pain level, she realized she felt a whole lot better. She checked her cell phone. It was now past eight. Grabbing another two plus hours helped her feel relatively decent. Now if only she had clothes to get changed into. She had to stay in the bathrobe and oversize T-shirt that had been provided for her.

She slipped her feet into slippers on the floor beside the bed and walked to the chair to put on the bathrobe. In the bathroom once again, she straightened up her tangled mess of auburn curls but gave up. She'd have to use a lot of conditioner to get the curls under control. She wasn't even sure that was possible at this point as a shower was out of the question for now.

She walked to the door, feeling more energetic. Although various parts of her body hurt, the pains weren't sharp in her back. She opened the door and stepped out in the hallway.

Once again it was empty. But this time she remembered her way to the elevator, taking it to the main floor, and headed for the kitchen. She stopped when she saw Alfred's face focused on the large grill in front of him, busy cooking up what appeared to be food for dozens of people. Instinctively she walked forward and asked, "May I help you?"

He looked up and smiled at her. "You can help me by going in and sitting down beside Dakota. He's been worried about you."

"I can do that," she said gently. "But I can also help you. I'm not helpless, and I'm not that badly injured."

He shook his head. "I've got this."

She admired his efficiency as he worked his way from one side of the grill to the other. "You do have my utmost admiration. It takes skill to cook for this many people all the time."

"You grow into it."

"I wonder." She made her way through the kitchen to the dining room.

Dakota hopped to his feet. "I was hoping you'd sleep in longer."

"I woke up a few moments ago. I didn't feel comfortable as a guest to just stay in bed."

"That's hardly an issue here. Until you're back to full health, sleep in as long as you want. It's important we take care of you and make sure you're safe." He pulled out a chair and said, "Sit down. I'll get you a cup of coffee."

She managed to sit on her own and settled back slightly. If she kept her position and posture relaxed and in good form, the pain wasn't too severe. And of course everybody else was checking her out too. She smiled at the people around the table a little shyly. There were more women now than she remembered seeing last night, but then last night she couldn't identify one from the other. "Good morning, everyone," she said.

"Good morning" was the chorus answer.

Ice walked in just then, studied Bailey carefully and said, "You look much better."

"Thank you. I'm feeling a bit better." When Dakota placed a cup of coffee in front of her, she smiled her thanks and turned her attention back to Ice. "Any word from the detective?"

Ice said, "He didn't find anything this morning either because of the heavy rains."

Beside her, Dakota opened several images and then turned his laptop for her to see. She studied the men's faces. One image showed two men, the mayor stood in the center. Standing beside the mayor was the man who had shot the third man.

She tapped the man's face on the screen and said, "That's the man who shot the third one."

"That's Jim Haskell," Dakota said. "One of the mayor's two right-hand men." He brought up a third image and said, "This is the third man that made up their very strong trio. His name is Troy Burgess."

She stared at it, felt the click of recognition and whispered in a low tone, "Not strong enough. That's the man who was shot."

OF ALL THE things to come out of her mouth, that was not what he had expected. He didn't realize she'd been so close that she could see the victim's face. No wonder they'd shot at her. And wouldn't stop looking for her either. On a whim, he had brought up the third man. He studied her drawn features. "Are you sure?"

Her gaze flicked back to the image, and she nodded. "I'm sure."

He turned to the others. "Now what?"

Ice already had her phone out, dialing Detective Mannford. She stood up and stepped away from the crowd, so she could hear better. When Mannford answered the phone, she spoke. "This is Ice. We have a tentative ID on the victim."

She continued to walk away, making it hard for anybody to hear the rest of the conversation. But it wasn't hard to see Bailey's reaction. She reached out a trembling hand to pick up her coffee cup but put it down because she couldn't stop the liquid from spilling over the edge. She clenched her hands into fists and rested them on her lap.

Dakota reached over and covered her hands with his. "It'll be fine."

She raised her dark gaze to his. "A man died."

"And you couldn't have done anything to stop it," he said, his voice gentle with understanding. "You can't take on the guilt for that."

She bit on her lip and then slowly nodded. "Intellectually I know that's true. But emotionally I'm still kind of wrecked about it. I stood there and stared when I should've cried for help. I should've done something. What if he wasn't killed outright by the bullet? What if he died later because he didn't get help fast enough?"

"With a bullet taken at such a close distance in the chest area of the body, chances are he was dead before he hit the ground."

She shrugged. "And again I know that in theory, but …" She sighed. "The police need to check that I have the right man."

Ice returned to the table. "Mannford is doing just that first thing. If he can't find him, he'll put out an APB for him. Then he'll visit the mayor."

"And still it's my word against theirs," Bailey said. "And I'm no one."

Levi nodded. "Exactly why you must stay out of sight. If

you are the only witness who can prove their involvement, then it will be to their benefit if you disappear."

She took a low gasping breath.

Ice added, "And considering they have already taken one life, they won't stop at taking a second."

Bailey swallowed hard. "I can take the vacation and sick days I've accrued at my job," she said hesitantly. "But after that expires, I have to return to work. My husband's illness wiped out our savings."

The others exchanged a look. Dakota knew what they were thinking. It wouldn't be a case of a week or two. She would pretty well have to stay out of sight for a long time. At least until after this was settled one way or another.

He glanced across at Ice. "Witness protection?"

She raised an eyebrow and tilted her head to the side as if considering. "I'll bring it up with Mannford when we get that far. Let's hope there's a much faster, easier solution than that."

Bailey stared at Dakota in shock. "No way I can do something like that."

He glanced over at her. "You're already alone. You've lost the person who mattered the most to you, and you have no other good friends or family. Right now witness protection would be easy. New name, new location. You're already doing that right now."

She opened her mouth to protest and slowly closed it. "It just seems wrong."

He shook his head. "Unfortunately many people have gone through something like this."

"But that's not today's issue," Ice said firmly. "I need to check your dressing. We can do it now or after you've eaten."

Alfred's voice called from the kitchen, "Breakfast is ready."

Everybody bolted into action, some setting the table, others walking into the kitchen to help Alfred carry out the trays of food.

Dakota sat beside Bailey. "Just sit tight."

He watched the amazement cross her face as the group played a part in bringing out platters of food and plates and cutlery, not to mention the condiments they each wanted.

When a large platter of unbuttered toast came out, she smiled. "That's something I can do to help."

A large container of butter and a knife were handed to her with a plate. She quickly worked her way through the job. Within minutes everybody sat at the table, joking and talking as they served themselves the delicious food. She snagged a piece of toast before the platter moved on to the next person. Dakota made sure all the other dishes came by her, and she had a decent selection for herself. She needed sustenance to regain her strength and to heal.

"What kind of work do you do in town?" Ice asked.

"I'm a buyer for Waltons, Inc. It's a restaurant supply house."

Several people nodded around the table, understanding what she did.

Dakota wasn't exactly sure. "Does that mean you do all the purchasing for the company?"

She nodded. "Yes, I source the best prices and then do all the ordering and budgeting for the company."

"Do you like the job?" Ice asked.

"It keeps me busy, not having time to think about missing my husband. A lot of work is involved, and I like that. I work mostly alone, and that's also not necessarily a bad thing. All in all, it's a good job."

"Was this a new job after your husband passed away?" Dakota asked.

"Yes, I've only been there almost six months." She shot him a look. "How did you know?"

"Because you don't have much time off coming to you."

She nodded. "I lost my job when my husband became so ill. But I had to turn around and get another one quickly. Of course it was temporary with no benefits. Though, at that time, I ended up with about four different jobs." Bailey shrugged. "The only thing I hated about that was how I was away from him for hours. ... When he passed away, I had to sell everything to cover the bills. It took me a long time to clear it all." She gave a ghost of a smile. "I know I should be proud I'm debt-free again, but honestly it was a hard go. And I don't want to go through it again so soon."

There was silence as everyone contemplated the burden on her shoulders. She'd been dealing with it the best she could.

"The fact that you've cleared yourself of those debts says a lot," Sienna said. "It takes a massive amount of dedication and savings to do that."

"All I had was work," Bailey admitted. "I took all the overtime I could get."

Ice winced. "It probably took plenty to pay for his last months in the hospital, so that made it almost impossible for you to stay home."

Bailey nodded. "I had to work. His medication was extremely expensive, and I couldn't see him suffer without it. So not working wasn't an option."

"You survived. That's what counts. Your husband would want you to have a whole new life now. And tomorrow will look brighter than today yet again."

"Right, I just saw somebody murdered. The killers saw me and tried to kill me. You almost ran me down with your SUV, and I ended up in the hospital," she snapped sarcastically. "How is that better?" Almost instantly she felt bad about her outburst. "Sorry, Dakota. You don't deserve that." She glanced at her watch. "I should phone my company to let them know I need a few days medical leave."

"Will that cause problems for you?" Levi asked from the head of the table.

"I don't think so. I have maybe five days' worth of sick leave and vacation time, six maybe. I'd have to check. I'm definitely not capable of working, so, with a medical excuse, I should be fine. Although I might need a note from my doctor. And that could get a little bit embarrassing. I don't really want people to know what happened."

"We actually can't have you telling anybody either. Once the police report is filed, it's not something you want to share."

She nodded, pushed her empty plate back. "Alfred is an awesome cook."

"He is."

"If you'll excuse me, I'll go phone my company." She pushed her chair back and froze as the pain had her hunching over and gasping for breath. Instantly Dakota hopped to his feet and gently eased her chair back so she could stand.

"Easy," he said.

Biting her lip, she slowly pulled herself vertical and walked, albeit stiffly, down to the far end of the room by the window. He watched as she pulled out her phone and made the call.

He hated to say it, but he really wished he could hear her

conversation. He had no reason to disbelieve her, but he hadn't gotten this far in life without being cynical to a certain extent.

"She's lovely," Ice said.

"She is. I just wish I knew more about her."

"Didn't you do research last night?"

"Yes, and everything seems on the up-and-up."

"Seems?" Merk asked from the far side of the table. "Is your instinct telling you something's off?"

"I don't understand why she paused at the alleyway in the first place."

"Surely it's not that dangerous an area that anybody can't walk down an alley?" Sienna said. "I often walk through places you guys wouldn't like."

Rhodes turned to look at her. "You what?"

She raised an eyebrow in challenge. "I like alleyways. They're full of character."

Rhodes walked over to her. "We have to talk."

She snickered. "But it will only end up the way it did the last time we *talked*."

Dakota watched in amusement as color washed up Rhodes's neck. He quickly grabbed his coffee and took a sip and refused to join in the conversation.

It was Ice who said, "If you have any questions you need answered, then we should get them answered now before we get too far down this road."

He nodded. "I thought I'd take her back to the alley and have her act out the steps she took, how she would've been positioned, where the murder took place, and then I'd look for any evidence. I can also swing by her apartment and grab some of her clothes." He shot another glance to where she talked earnestly on the phone in the distance and added,

"The only thing is, I'm not sure she should be doing that much traveling."

Ice paused as she considered it. "As long as it's just the drive and walking around a little bit, and she's very careful getting in and out of the vehicle, she should be fine. But she'll need to make sure she has her painkillers. Then she comes back here and lies down again. But watch your back. She's a target. That makes you one too. Merk will go with you."

"It's at the edge of town. So forty minutes to wherever the location was, twenty minutes to half an hour maximum to get her back to her house, grab her bag, and then home again."

"Do it then," Levi said. "Check in with me when you're back."

Chapter 6

A FTER PUTTING AWAY her phone, Bailey carefully made her way back to the table. Several people stood, so she wasn't sure she should sit down again or if she was to go back to her room.

Dakota stepped in front of her and asked, "How are you feeling?"

She gave the question some serious thought. "I've been better, but I'm actually not feeling too bad. When I turn the wrong way, it often takes a few minutes for the flare-up to calm down, but overall I'm okay. Why?"

"I want to take you back to your place to get some clothes."

She grinned. "Oh, I think I can manage a trip for that."

"You probably shouldn't go," he stressed. "Any movement will slow healing so, you have to promise not to do too much."

"You don't have to worry about that. Even sitting hurts, and I just don't understand how that could be."

"Your whole body comes into play with an injury like that. While we're out, I would like to drive past the alley and look at the actual location and layout of the crime you saw."

"It probably would be a good idea for me to go back and look too. I don't know how hazy my memories are, how much shock plays into them." She glanced down at the bathrobe she wore. "I'm also extremely short on clothes. I can wear my pants again but I don't have a clean shirt."

Sienna stood up and looked at her. "I have a light-blue T-shirt that's sure to fit you and is really soft so should feel nice against your stitches, if you would like to borrow that."

Bailey smiled. "Thank you. I'd really appreciate it."

The three of them went back upstairs with Sienna heading off down the hallway to her room. She returned a moment later with the light-blue cotton T-shirt. "Try this."

They were almost at Bailey's doorway. She accepted the shirt and said, "Thank you. I'll try it on." Facing Dakota now, she said, "Give me five minutes to get dressed."

Inside she sat down slowly on the bed. Her back really was killing her. She counted the hours and realized it was time for another painkiller. She reached for the bottle, took them and the antibiotics as instructed, swallowing them down with a drink of water.

She straightened a bit and tugged the T-shirt nightgown up and over her head and cried out, but she managed to get it off.

She wasn't sure she could wear a bra. She walked into the bathroom and checked the height of the bandage with the mirror. It would be close, but maybe Ice could lower the bandage or at least adjust it so the bra strap wouldn't interfere. She brushed her hair and then tried on the bra, followed by the borrowed T-shirt.

It was a perfect fit. She fingered the lightweight material and smiled. It was supersoft, like a stroke of kindness on her skin. Dressed and unable to make the bed without causing more pain, she slowly opened the door to find Dakota waiting for her. "I put these clothes on, but the socks and shoes," she confessed, "were beyond me."

He nodded and stepped into her room, looking at the shoes. "You need socks for these?"

She glanced down at the low-slung ballet shoes. "Maybe that would be a better answer." She quickly stepped into them and smiled. "We won't do too much walking, so they should be fine."

With him at her side, they walked to the SUV. Forty minutes later they approached the outskirts of town. She had taken a few minutes to get her bearings as it wasn't an area she was accustomed to entering town from. With a few directions, she sent him back to the corner where she had seen the shooting. She didn't like the idea of walking the area, but there was no other way to make sure nothing was left to find.

He walked around and helped her from the SUV. Merk stood watch.

"Exactly where were you just before the shooting?"

She motioned to the main side of the block. He strode with her to where she'd been standing and carefully led her through the steps she'd taken.

"I came in the alleyway here, and that's when I saw the men. I kept walking, and then I heard the shot."

He stopped and stared at her. "No, that doesn't work. You said the men were inside the alley down here."

She nodded. "I thought I heard something first and so had stepped in a little bit to see what was going on. But when I saw the three men in their business suits, I just turned and walked away."

He studied her face for a long moment.

Inside she felt everything go still. He didn't believe her, or did he? She bit the inside of her lip. "No, that's not right. I thought I saw something on the ground."

"What you mean, *something?*"

She walked back to the opening of the alleyway and pointed to where some crumpled paper was. "I thought it was money."

He walked over to see the green and white paper and nodded. "Now that makes sense."

She stood where the paper was. "I turned to look down the alley and had a much better view."

"So, from here, you saw the three men standing where?"

She pointed at the location. "But, once I realized it wasn't money, I hurriedly left, and that was when I heard the shot." She paused. "No, I heard them shouting," she corrected herself. "I turned around, and that's when I saw the gun raised, and the tall man shot the third man. I up and bolted."

"Which direction did you run?"

She pointed to the corner up ahead. "I cut across the traffic and went through that block."

He turned and studied where she'd run and realized it was a straight line of sight. He nodded. "Okay, so that's when he shot you. And you carried on down the block a little bit. I was two blocks away when you ran into me."

She nodded.

He walked a little more into the alley. "Am I standing where the men were standing?"

She frowned and studied the angle. "I only had a really fast glimpse of them." She pursed her lips. "A little more to the right."

He stepped to where she said.

She nodded. "I think the three of them were there."

She walked closer to him. He stopped and slowly looked around on the ground. Mud still covered the alleyway, but it had dried up considerably. The ground had been thirsty for water and, although it was still wet on the surface, it was quickly disappearing.

He reached for a soggy cigarette butt.

"How can you tell if that's recent?" she asked.

"After the rain, it's hard to say. For all I know, this is Detective Mannford's."

She couldn't imagine a detective leaving evidence in a crime scene.

But accidents happened. Dakota spent ten minutes looking around the area but found no evidence of a shooting. If there had been blood, it'd been washed away in the downpour. There weren't even footprints left that matched the scenario. Finally he straightened and smiled at her. "Okay, let's head to your apartment."

She smiled with relief. "Good. I don't like it here."

"Understandable." He led her toward the SUV, helping her once again back inside.

Her apartment wasn't very far away. When they pulled up to the front of the building, there was an odd sense of loneliness. It hadn't been a happy place for her once Rick got ill. It was the same apartment she'd shared with her husband. They'd been together for so little time before he'd been diagnosed. The pain and sadness and grief overrode the good memories. And for that she was sorry. She'd had a lovely six months with him while he was healthy.

With Merk sitting in the SUV, keeping watch and waiting for them, they walked to the entrance. At the door to her apartment, she quickly unlocked the door and pushed it open. "I shouldn't need too long," she said stepping inside. "I just want to get like a week's worth of clothing."

He grabbed her arm, and she was jerked to a standstill.

She shot him a look, and he motioned toward the apartment. She spun around and gasped. "Oh, my God."

Her apartment had been trashed.

GRIMLY DAKOTA SURVEYED the living space. This hadn't been a robbery; this had been a message. There wasn't a couch cushion, a wall, a foot of flooring that wasn't either damaged or tossed with paint or in some other way destroyed. He quickly walked through to the bedroom to see the same thing. In the bathroom, he stopped to see lipstick on the mirror that read *Keep your mouth shut, bitch*. He pulled out his phone, quickly updated Merk and took pictures.

Bailey hadn't seen this yet.

He joined her as they walked through the apartment systematically, taking pictures of the damage. He sent them all to Ice and glanced over at Bailey, but she stood in the hall, leaning against the wall, tears in her eyes and her arms wrapped around her chest. Not frozen but daunted by the task in front of her.

He walked over and nudged her chin up. "We need to see if you have any usable clothes left for you to grab."

She shook her head. "My God, why vandalize my place like this?"

"The people you saw in the alley are sending a warning to keep you from talking."

She closed her eyes briefly, then straightened, turned and walked into the bedroom. He helped her find her travel bag among the mess. The vandals had cut the top so the zipper would no longer close, but it would still do for their purposes. If there was anything left to pack. She didn't have much.

Her shirts were cut; things had been ripped off their hangers, and most were damaged from the paint tossed on top.

She glanced around. "I don't think anything here is salvageable."

There was so much pain in her voice. This woman who had already lost so damn much, had paid the price for so much and now was faced with the complete ruination of all personal effects in her apartment.

"Do you have anything of your husband's you want to take?"

She looked at him, startled, and walked over to the night table. It had been pulled out, but underneath was a stack of books, still sitting as if untouched. She pulled out the very bottom one and opened it to show a keepsake box. Inside were their wedding rings, several photos, some folded pieces of paper. She clutched it against her chest. "This is the only thing I need from here. It's the only thing worth keeping."

He nodded. "We have to phone the police, make a report for this for insurance." He winced at his next thought. "Did you have insurance for your contents?"

She looked up at him and shook her head. In a soft voice she whispered, "No. There was no money left over for that. Everything I have is old, used. I sold everything but my business clothes for my job. Then, when I lost that job, it didn't matter. I could wear casual clothing to my temporary jobs and at my current position." She looked at the bed. The mattress had been tossed and destroyed. "I can replace everything at a second-hand store. I don't have the funds yet, but it shouldn't take too long to get up enough to start again. The clothes are really what I needed the most." She glanced down at the paint strewn on top of everything. "I just don't know where to begin."

Dakota took a serious look. It was almost as if the intruders had deliberately made sure every piece of clothing was destroyed. The dresser was still standing, but the drawers were left open; several drawers were missing, dumped on the floor. Inside he was swearing heavily. It took a real asshole to destroy what little she had left.

Beside him, she said with a humorous note in her tone, "The only good thing about this is, I don't have much left to move." And she turned resolutely and left the bedroom.

Dakota watched her walk over a few piles of cushions and knickknacks as she went into the kitchen, where dishes had been dumped, the food jars shattered. On the counter, written in what looked like spaghetti sauce, was the word *Bitch*. She stared at it for a long time. "They must be really afraid of what I have to say."

"Terrified."

She wrapped her arms around her chest. "Could we please go to the nearest department store? I'll pick up a few necessities for the next couple days."

As they went to the front door, she paused. She looked in the coat closet, but every jacket had been pulled out and knifed several times.

She didn't say a word. She just slowly exited the apartment.

Outside in the hallway, Dakota's phone rang. It was Ice.

"You get whatever she needs in town for a few days. Detective Mannford can see to the apartment."

"We just have to report this to the superintendent here. She's only renting."

"Okay. But, before you leave town, Mannford wants to talk to you."

"I'll call him next."

While Bailey watched, Dakota dialed Detective Mannford. Bailey walked over to the window at the end of the hall and stared out at the world around her.

Dakota put away his phone. "We need to wait for Detective Mannford."

She bowed her head. "That's fine. We should talk to the super."

She led the way back downstairs to the main floor to the last apartment and knocked on the door. An older man answered. When they explained what happened, he shook his head and wanted her contact information. Dakota gave it to him instead and said, "Detective Mannford from the police department is on his way here. They'll be upstairs taking pictures so we can file a report."

The super nodded. "I'll need a copy of that report for the owners." And he closed the door on them.

Chapter 7

B AILEY HADN'T SEEN too much human kindness in the last couple years. But even the super's attitude was cold, disinterested. It was hard to stomach.

As they walked back to the main entranceway to take the elevator again, the detective walked in. He studied her face carefully. "How are you doing?"

"Moving slowly but holding up."

Upstairs in the apartment, he stopped at the open door and stared. He glanced over at Dakota.

Dakota nodded. "It's pretty bad in there."

Bailey just couldn't imagine anybody taking the time to so thoroughly destroy every single thing she owned.

"It's certainly not good," Detective Mannford said. He took a walk through the apartment, came back and said, "I know it's probably a foolish question, but do you know if anything's missing?"

She stared at him in surprise. "I couldn't tell. But I didn't have anything worth taking, so I doubt it."

"TV? There's no TV here."

"I don't have one. I couldn't afford one anymore."

"Camera, electronics?"

She shook her head. "No, I have a tablet, but it's in my purse. That's it. Again I couldn't afford any of that stuff."

He nodded and kept walking through the apartment.

Finally he returned again. "I'll get the report written up. Then you can sign it. We'll give you copies so you can give them to your insurance company."

At that Dakota stepped up. "She doesn't have any contents insurance for her personal belongings."

The detective sighed. "I'm really sorry. This is a blow."

"It's a blow, but it would've been much worse if I'd been here at the time."

He smiled at her in approval. "That is very true."

Detective Mannford took care of formalities while they were here. He made short work of interviewing her about what she'd seen. At least unofficially.

When they were done, so was she. It was obvious. Dakota was more than a little worried about her.

"Did you take your medication this morning?" he asked.

She nodded. "But now you can tell it's wearing off. I need my antibiotics." She glanced at her watch. "It's almost two already."

"You want to go for lunch or you want to go straight home?"

She glanced over at him. "*Home* is an odd word for me to use."

"For the moment, your home is where I live."

She smiled. "Thank you. It would be very nice. I would like to go straight home."

He helped her back into the truck, nodded to Merk and placed a call to Ice with an update. "We're coming home."

THE DRIVE BACK was short and sweet. By the time they got there, Bailey had fallen asleep. He pulled inside the garage and turned off the engine. Merk already had her door open.

Then Dakota walked around to her side. "Bailey? Bailey, we're here. Wake up, honey."

She mumbled but turned to the other side to get away from his voice, disturbing her sleep. He didn't want to give her a shake because that would likely hurt her back.

He shifted the seat slightly to get an arm underneath her. And then he picked her up in his arms, trying to avoid the main part of her back, and walked inside the house with her, Merk holding open the door for them.

Alfred came running. "Is she hurt?"

Dakota shook his head. "No. She just fell asleep about ten minutes ago. Apparently she held out as long as she could. She should be out for hours."

Alfred took over for Merk and went ahead of Dakota and Bailey, leading the way upstairs to her room. Alfred pulled down the blankets, smoothed her bed and moved the bathrobe and nightgown so Dakota could lay her down.

Gently Dakota placed her on the bed, slipped off her shoes and pulled the covers over her. He stepped back to where Alfred stood in the doorway. "Hopefully she'll get a couple hours rest."

He headed back downstairs, and his phone rang. He grabbed it, not knowing the number, and answered it.

A hard cold voice said, "We want the girl. Name the time and place."

And the caller hung up.

Chapter 8

BAILEY WOKE UP hot, uncomfortable and cranky as hell. She lay in the bed for a long moment, realizing where she was and where she could no longer be. She didn't have a bed of her own that was usable anymore. What had happened to her life?

She threw back the covers and just lay there for a few minutes. She was fully dressed. It seemed Dakota had carried her to bed; the last thing she remembered was the drive home.

What she really wanted was a shower. But again she didn't know if that was possible with her stitches. The other thing she needed, and in a bad way, were her painkillers.

She propped herself up on her elbow and took both her pills again. She glanced at her phone and realized it was almost 5:00 p.m. She shook her head. "Where has the day gone?"

She forced herself vertical and headed to the bathroom. There she took the washcloth and towel, and did as thorough a wash job as possible. After brushing her hair with the small brush from her purse, she felt marginally better. Knowing they would all be downstairs for dinner, she slowly made her way to the door and down the hall.

When she walked into the dining room, silence fell. She stood quiet for a long moment, then said, "Did I do something wrong?"

Ice stood up. "No, you certainly didn't."

Just then Dakota and Levi walked in from the garage, both talking. Levi saw her first.

She gave him a small smile. "Hello."

Dakota caught sight of her and smiled. He walked over and held out an arm for her. She grasped it gratefully. She didn't think she needed the physical support, but she realized the emotional one was a crutch she would have a hard time letting go of.

"Did you get some sleep?"

She nodded and laughed. "And you must have carried me to bed, though I don't even remember that happening, so I presume I slept well."

With his help, she made her way to the same chair she'd sat in earlier.

As soon as she sat down, Ice placed a cup of coffee in front of her, taking a long moment to study her features, seeing the shakiness of her hands. Ice motioned at the coffee. "Drink up. And if you can stand it with sugar, that would be good for you."

"I don't normally like coffee at all," she confessed. "Maybe I will try it once with sugar." The sugar bowl arrived beside her, and she put a bit in. "And why do I need the sugar?"

"You still look pretty shaky."

Dakota reached over and laced his fingers with hers. "And you have another shock coming."

She froze and turned to look at him. "What else can there be?"

"I received a phone call from a stranger, telling me that they wanted you, and I was to name the time and place."

She stared straight ahead, feeling all her strength drain right down to her toes. She slumped in her chair and then straightened with a cry of pain. "Really? Seriously?"

He nodded. "Apparently they know you're with me."

She covered her mouth, holding back the cry threatening to come out. "That's terrible."

He shrugged. "Actually I'm not upset about it at all."

She gave a tiny headshake in confusion. "That makes no sense. Now you are a target too." She glanced around. "That means Mayor Alden has targeted this place." She tried to push her chair back. "I have to leave."

Dakota squeezed her hand, urging her to sit back down again. She slowly lowered herself and stared at him wordlessly.

"You're not leaving. You're staying here. If somebody wants to attack us, this is probably the best place you could possibly be. We've withstood attacks before."

Ice and Levi nodded. "Not that were looking for a fight, but, if it comes our way, you can bet we're ready for it."

Bailey stared at them in shock. "But don't you understand? They shot that man. They're looking to kill me."

Ice smiled and said, "We know that. We know exactly what you're up against. We've been in this situation many times before." She leaned over and gently covered Bailey's hand with hers, adding, "Every one of us here is prepared to fight."

Bailey opened her mouth to say something, but no words came out. She slowly closed her mouth, then said, "Are you serious?"

Levi nodded. "Ice and all the males in my compound are ex-military."

"And some of us have a lot of martial arts training," Sienna said. "I've got three brothers in the military, so this is nothing new for me. Besides several of us have been kidnapped, shot at and God-only-knows-whatever-else," she said with a chuckle. "It's a chance for a bit of payback."

Bailey let her gaze stray from one serious face to the next. Although humor was in the air, an underlining sense of determination that they were here for her was present as well. And, if that fight came to them, not a one of them would back down. In fact, she got the idea several of them were more than ready for that little bit of excitement in their world.

"I can't even imagine how impossible my life would be right now if I hadn't run into Dakota," she admitted. "Thank you so very much for believing me, for not putting me out in the cold."

"We don't do that. Loyalty, integrity and honesty. We value those above all else."

Levi grabbed Ice's hand. "Don't forget *love*. I might not discuss this much, but, if anything is worth fighting for—to the end of time, to have and to keep—it's love."

There was silence around the table for a long moment, and then someone at the far end said, "Amen to that."

She turned to look at Alfred and smiled. "You sure you can handle looking after one more person?" At his nod she added, "As soon as I can, I'm more than happy to help you. I've certainly spent enough years in the kitchen to claim experience."

He glanced at her in surprise. "I thought you were a buyer?"

She nodded. "I am now. I used to be a chef for one of the big golf course restaurants. I hurt my leg in a car accident, and I just couldn't handle the pace anymore. I didn't want to be standing in the kitchen twelve to sixteen hours a day. So I moved to restaurant supplies and now work at Waltons, Inc."

Alfred nodded. "As soon as you want to help, you just let me know. I will make room for you." He smiled and walked away. At the door, he paused and called back, "But you are not to set foot in my kitchen until the stitches are out. Do you hear me?"

She nodded with a smile on her face.

Then he added, "Dinner is served in twenty minutes."

She settled back and realized, to her astonishment, tears ran down her cheeks. Embarrassed, she picked up a napkin and hurriedly wiped her eyes. "I'm sorry."

In a low voice, Dakota said, "Don't be. We all know how you feel."

She turned to look at him and realized that he meant it. He really understood. He and his team had been through so much that they understood what another person came up against or had seen in the world. They understood where she was coming from right now. It made her feel as if he did know—a very comforting sensation.

DAKOTA KEPT AN eye on her, wishing he had his phone to continue his research. Only Merk had taken Dakota's phone to trace where the call had come from. But with no number and no name showing, chances were the call had been placed on a throwaway phone. What Dakota needed was to come up with a plan, but that would take the entire unit, not just him.

"Has anyone told Detective Mannford about Dakota's mystery call?" Bailey asked in a low tone.

Ice nodded. "I've contacted him already to let him know, but it doesn't change anything."

Bailey shook her head. "He shot at me. He destroyed my apartment. Now he makes a threatening phone call. That sounds like he's escalating."

Levi smiled at her. "It is what it is. So far, he's increasing pressure. Whether they actually saw you at the apartment today, I don't know, but I would presume not. Otherwise I would've expected them to attack both of you while you were there."

"Plus we had Merk out front. We weren't there for that long before the detective showed up. Maybe they didn't want to go against him," Dakota said. Inside he was pissed. "I wish they had shown up. I'd like a chance to fight back."

Rhodes said, "It's not like anybody does fifty paces at the edge of town anymore to settle a dispute. Now somebody goes out in the middle of the night and shoots somebody dead rather than argue. And the cops have to put the pieces together to figure out who did it."

"But, in this case, everybody knows who did it," Bailey said. "Why can't the detective pick him up and charge him?"

"As much as you're a witness, it'll be your word against his."

There was silence. She looked at them bewildered. "Is my word not good enough?"

Dakota reached over and squeezed her hand again. "It's not that. It's not good, but they will make it sound like you're incredibly depressed after losing your husband. You've lost all meaning in your life, and you're doing this to either gain attention or because you're off your depression medication of some kind. Whereas, on the other side, they'll have a prominent politician with a well-known public face and persona, and people will naturally believe him over you."

She stared at him in horror. "Are you serious? Why would anybody believe a politician?"

Levi chuckled. "Unfortunately those are the facts of life."

"I'm not depressed. Just want to point that out. Neither am I doing this to gain any attention. Honestly I'd much rather none of this had happened. I could be living in my nice quiet little place, thank you. It beats dealing with this crap," she muttered.

The others nodded in sympathy. "Boring and bland looks good after bullets," Sienna said. "The thing is, we've all been through something similar, so you're in the right place."

Bailey grinned at her. "I know it's wrong to think this way, but I have to admit that I'm kind of glad you guys understand. I'm just terribly sorry for putting you in this position."

"What we must do," Dakota said beside her, "is make sure they can't get to you here."

Her gaze searched the faces around her. "Are you really thinking they'll attack this place?"

"It's hard to say. They could put a sniper on the hills out here and wait for you to come out."

Instantly she felt sick to her stomach. She pulled her hand away from Dakota's and slouched back and then straightened immediately as her back screamed at her. She rubbed her temple. "I don't think the way you think. I can't even imagine living in a world where snipers might shoot people from the hills around here."

"However, we do think that way, and so do the killers," Ice said carefully. "Which is also why we have security cameras all over the hills around us for that very reason."

Dakota watched as Bailey's mouth dropped open. He forgot what it was like to live a civilian life, not dealing with all this subterfuge and warfare, especially hidden warfare. For Bailey, this was a foreign world, and he could understand her shock and confusion. "The thing to remember is that we do understand how all this works," he said firmly. "We'll do the best we can to keep you safe."

"And what about keeping yourself safe?" She motioned at Sienna. "She has the same color hair as I do. What if she steps out of the compound and a sniper shoots her instead of me?" she cried out. "I can't live with that." She glanced over at Sienna to see Rhodes reaching across the table to grab Sienna's hand.

Bailey nodded. "See? You matter to him. I don't matter to anybody. If my life is snuffed out, it makes not one bit of difference to anybody in this world. My company will hire a new buyer within days. My apartment is already not inhabitable until they can fix it up. There is no reason for anybody else to sacrifice themselves to save me. I'm a mouse in a world full of wolves and foxes." She stared at them all helplessly. "Please don't let yourself get hurt to save me."

There was silence all around the room. Dakota didn't even know what to say. Her description of her own life was breathtakingly sad. That she could see herself in that light and think she had so little value because nobody loved her, because nobody was there for her ... was a glimpse into her world that hurt.

"That may have been your life for this last year and a half," he said in a flat voice, "but, before that, there were people who loved you."

"And those people are gone. If I'm to die because of some asshole politician, and I can't do anything about it myself, that's one thing. But to have somebody else get hurt and possibly die because of me, that just is not acceptable." She shook her head. "I mean it. I refuse to let you do anything that will put somebody here in harm's way."

Levi looked at her with interest. "How do you plan to stop us?"

She glared at him. "I'll leave. I'll walk out that door all alone, and whoever wants to take me out, let them."

She said it so simply, so breathtakingly honest he sat back and stared at her. "You can't give up your life for something like this."

She turned on him fiercely. "I will not stand by while somebody else I know suffers because of me. I loved my husband. I did anything and everything I could to keep him alive. If I could have sacrificed myself to give him just one more month, I would have done so without thinking."

Dakota glared at her. "And did you ever think, from your husband's point of view, how that would make him feel? How incredibly guilty he'd feel? He would hate himself that you would sacrifice your healthy body and your healthy future for one month for his crippled body to live." He stared at her, surprised at the anger inside of him. "You may think you're being selfless, but that's actually being incredibly selfish. Because you would've sacrificed yourself, thinking you were doing the right thing, but all you would have done was save yourself the pain of losing him. And taking that pain and turning it on him would have been twice as bad."

She stared at him, her hand covering her mouth, tears welling up in her eyes.

And instantly he felt like a heel. His anger drained away. He shook his head. "I'm sorry. I had no right to say that."

Just then Alfred walked in with platters of food and

filled the table.

Dakota could feel her trembling in shock from his words, maybe just the entire scenario making her whole body shake. He also knew the way she was cringing in the chair away from him that he was the last person she wanted in her world. And that was too damn bad. He'd inflicted this hurt; he had to heal it. If he could.

He filled her plate and in a neutral tone of voice said, "Eat. You can't even walk out of here until you're strong enough."

She fought back a sob, immediately slapping her hand over her mouth. He was sorry for what he had said—or at least sorry for having said it in such an irate tone and so publicly. But he meant it. If he'd been her husband, he would've been horrified for her to do something like that.

The table resumed general conversation to pull the attention away from her. He knew everybody was keeping an eye on her, and that had to be hard. He poured her a glass of water, then nudged her gently and said, "Eat."

Chapter 9

B AILEY SLOWLY STRAIGHTENED, grabbed her napkin, wiped her eyes, blew her nose and then picked up her fork. She couldn't escape easily with her injured back. The effort to move quickly would cause her more damage. The only thing she could do was get through this. And she had to do it without examining his words. Because they hurt. Every word was like a sword to her heart. He didn't understand— he didn't really know what it was like to watch somebody you love die in front of you. She did, and she'd have done anything she could to stop it. But there was no stopping it. That incorrigible, encroaching, unforgiving death marched ever forward.

She looked up to find him holding a glass of water in front of her. She grabbed it and drank half of it down. She looked at the plate of food, and, although she was sick inside and out, she knew she needed this for energy. She stabbed a piece of broccoli and took a bite. That her mood made it taste like sawdust wasn't the issue. Alfred had gone to a tremendous amount of work to make this meal for so many people. All she could do was realize that her problem with Dakota was not the same problem with everybody. They had done so much to keep her safe, and even now they were doing the best they could. She needed to grow up and get over herself.

She sat quietly for several moments and then raised her head and smiled at Alfred. "Alfred, you're a genius."

He gave her a fatherly smile. "I'm glad you're enjoying it. Do you want seconds?"

She looked down at her plate and wondered if there was any room and then shook her head. "I don't think I could get another bite down."

"You might want to rethink that because I made cheese-cake today."

She let the corners of her mouth kick up. "Wow, cheese-cake. Normally I'd be all over it, but I'm full."

He leaned forward, a big grin on his face. "Even if it's lemon curd?"

She stared at him in delight. "Really? Fresh lemons?"

"That's the only way, my dear."

She gave him a big fat smile. "Yes, please."

With that, the rest of the table relaxed and settled into a more natural atmosphere.

Deliberately avoiding Dakota, she muttered out loud, "I'm sorry for my outburst. I do apparently have strong feelings about that subject."

Several chuckles came around the table. "We all have strong feelings about something. You did what you could for your husband. That's all that needs to be said."

She nodded, picked up the water and finished the rest of it. Her plate was empty, but the others still ate. She desperately wanted a cup of coffee, like she'd had last time with sugar, but it was behind her, and she didn't dare maneuver her sore body in that direction. She settled back to wait until everybody had finished eating.

She'd no sooner decided to relax and wait, when a hot cup of coffee arrived beside her. Dakota again—once more looking after her, seeing to her needs before she even noticed she had any. She gave a heavy sigh and muttered, "Sorry."

In an equally low voice he said, "Never say you're sorry. Your enemies won't believe you, and your friends don't need you to."

She smiled. "That might be true, but it's still nice to hear when you've done wrong. Or when you've been wronged." She looked up at him and smiled. "Forgive me?"

He flashed a wicked grin at her. "Nothing to forgive. When you love, you love deeply, and that's something we would all want."

She nodded and stayed quiet for the rest of the meal. She thought back to all the years when she'd worked as a chef. She'd loved food, had loved cooking for crowds, but somewhere along the line she got soured on the super wealthy patrons and the snotty chef she had worked with and the owners who had become way too difficult and demanding. The stress of it had been excruciating. Then she'd been injured.

Rick had asked her to quit. While they were still dating, he'd seen how damaging it all had been to her. And because of that, she'd taken the monumental step of walking away from her career, from her education and her love of cooking. She spent a lot of time feeding Rick his favorite dishes, and she slowly learned to rejoice again in food as a passion.

But, after his death, she completely walked away from it again. All food tasted like sawdust, and all her efforts to cook or eat had been way too much.

As she stared at the table in front of her, she realized she hadn't walked away as much as she stuffed it down deep inside. She could work at some place like this. She could do something like what Alfred did. Or work with somebody like

Alfred. A place where the stress wasn't hers alone, where the threat of being fired wasn't constantly on her mind, where she wouldn't have to work sixteen hours a day every day without a break.

She didn't mind being a buyer. She dealt with restaurant food supplies, so it was certainly her field, but she'd chosen an isolated job because she didn't have to reintegrate into society.

Going through what she'd gone through with her husband had meant stepping back from the world. Feeling isolated and alone as death marched to the end. Without a support group around her, she hadn't known how to re-enter society again. She'd been living in the cold and didn't know how to come back indoors.

Until Dakota. He hadn't given her a choice. He dragged her kicking and screaming into this world she found herself. It was foreign. But just like the other world had been foreign and she'd slowly gotten used to it, she could get used to this one too. Only she had no reason to stay here and being here meant putting them all in danger. And that was the sad truth. Yet she needed to find a purpose in her life again. In a way getting out of debt had been a big one. She'd skimped and saved, and she put every penny against Rick's medical debts. Thankfully selling off their assets had gone a long way to knocking it down before he died. Now that she was clear, she was homeless. Where did she go from here?

"Thoughts?" Dakota asked.

"Just wondering what I'm supposed to do with my life now."

"You take care of the present," he said. "The future will take care of itself."

She smiled. "That sounds like an adage my grandfather

would've said."

"Who was he?" Sienna asked from several seats away.

"He was an old shoemaker when the profession still existed," she said with a smile. "He was full of sayings like that."

DAKOTA ENJOYED LISTENING to her talk about her grandfather. She rambled on at an easy pace, telling stories of how he had raised his grandkids. Her parents had died young, leaving her and her baby brother. Her brother died of cancer when she was a young teen. If it hadn't been for her grandfather, she wouldn't have survived that either. Dakota was amazed at how often bad luck or tragedy seemed to follow some people. She was due for some good times. She might not believe that such a thing was possible, but he knew this crap life didn't last forever. He'd lost good friends in the military. Healing took time, but it did happen. One never forgot, but it became easier.

When Alfred brought out a huge cheesecake and set it down almost in front of her, she giggled with delight. "You weren't kidding. Lemon curd cheesecake." Immediately she launched into a discussion about what kinds of cheesecake she had tried to make before.

"I think by now," Alfred said with a smile, "I've tried every citrus there is."

"I've never tried grapefruit. Always wanted to."

Alfred looked thoughtful. "You know? I'm not sure I ever tried that either. I wonder if that would work."

She gave him a wicked glance. "If you have any, we could make one together tomorrow."

He grinned a smile that went from cheek to cheek as the

two both realized they were kindred souls. And maybe this was a good thing.

The cheesecake was quickly cut and dispersed among the group at the large table. Considering there were so many of them, the pieces were being fought over. Bailey took a small piece.

But at the first bite she closed her eyes and sank back in joy. "Alfred, you're a magician in the kitchen."

He chuckled but was obviously pleased, a nice rosy color came to his cheeks.

Dakota had never seen Alfred like this. And from the look in Ice and Levi's expressions, they hadn't either. The people here may be a strong family unit, but they had to remember not to take for granted any of the work any of them did. He took a bite of the cheesecake and stopped in shock at the explosion of flavor. "That's curd?"

Bailey chuckled. "That is lemon curd in cheesecake form. And it's divine."

With those words, Dakota dug into his piece and enjoyed it to the last bite. "You're right. That was spectacular." He sat back and rubbed his stomach. "That was an awesome meal, Alfred."

As people stood and collected the dishes like a well-oiled army, they headed into the kitchen to clean up.

Dakota noticed the tiredness on Alfred's face. He frowned. "Alfred, it's time you got some help in the kitchen."

Alfred shrugged. "There hasn't been any need until now."

"What he means is, he's refused until now," Ice said. "But it's past time. It's a huge workload for just him."

Beside him Bailey popped up, looking way too agile,

considering the stitches in her back. "I can help him for the next few days."

"No. Not with those stitches in your back, young lady."

She glared at him. "As long as I don't have to do any of the bending or heavy lifting, there's no reason I can't stand—or sit—at the island and do prep work."

He frowned and shook his head. "Better that you do nothing but lie in bed and relax."

She snickered at that. "I wouldn't know what to do with myself. I've been a workaholic since I was a child. That won't change now." And she collected the dishes around them, then carefully turned and gave the entire stack to Dakota.

He raised his eyebrows but didn't say a word and carried them into the kitchen.

In the background, he could hear Alfred squabbling with Ice over letting Bailey work in the kitchen.

Merk walked over and patted Dakota on the back. "Nice choice."

Dakota looked at him in surprise, but Merk was already on his way out of the room.

Rhodes chuckled. "Very good choice." And then he walked out.

Dakota had a good idea what was going on, but they were wrong. He was just helping a woman he'd accidentally hit.

Sienna stood beside Dakota, snickering. "You have no clue what's going on, do you?"

He glanced at her. "It's not like that."

She gave him a warm smile. "It's one of the unique things about this place. Somebody else always knows before the man does." And then she too turned and walked out.

Frowning, he rinsed the dishes and loaded them into the

commercial-size dishwasher. Little pots and pans remained, but they had a second dishwasher for those. Alfred, although he was still in the dining room, liked to put away the food himself.

By the time Dakota returned to the dining room to get another load, the table was already cleaned off. Alfred and Bailey had moved into a discussion of puddings.

"I do like making puddings with cream cheese," Bailey said.

"It makes it very rich."

She nodded. "Where I come from, that type of dessert is served in small elegant-looking portions."

Dakota leaned against a wall and watched, fascinated as she came to life, sitting right beside Alfred. Ice and Levi sat on the other end, studying the pair. Dakota didn't quite know where to go or what to do. He glanced at Levi, seeing the surprise in his face too.

Dakota grabbed a cup of coffee and sat down between the two groups. He didn't have any claim on Bailey, but he wanted to make sure she didn't stay up late. Besides, Alfred also looked tired, yet Dakota hated to remind him there was food to be put away. "Alfred, do you want me to deal with the leftovers?"

Alfred glanced at Dakota in surprise. "Oh, dear. I'll do that now." He hopped up from the table and walked around to the kitchen. On his heels was Bailey. As the two of them kept up the chatter in the kitchen, Dakota stood in the doorway and watched. Bailey quickly picked up on what Alfred was doing and got there before him, already saving the older man steps and movements. It said so much about who she was and how she had an innate sense about caring for people, whether her sick husband in the hospital or feeding large groups of people.

The others *were* right; she was a good choice. And he was an idiot because only now did he realize he was already seriously in trouble.

Ice walked up beside him, patted him on the back, and whispered, "I don't think I've ever seen Alfred so invigorated."

Dakota nodded. "Or Bailey."

She gave a soft chuckle and said, "Something for us all to think about." And she turned and walked out.

Dakota watched her leave, not sure what she meant by that.

Once the two were done putting away the food, Dakota told Alfred, "I'll make sure she lies down now. She probably did too much as it is."

Alfred shooed them away. "Go. Go lie down and rest."

Bailey had to be pulled from the kitchen and led toward the elevator. "I'm not that tired," she protested.

"Maybe not, but you've been up most of the day, moving around a lot of it. And your stitches probably need you to lie down again, okay?"

As they stood waiting for the elevator, Ice walked over to them. "Before you go, we should look at the bandage."

With a wince, Bailey obediently nodded and followed Ice downstairs to the medical clinic. There she stretched out on the bed and, although uncomfortable with some of her movements, she was no longer crying out in agony.

Ice lifted her shirt up her back and carefully took off the bandage.

Dakota studied the slash across the center of her back. "It doesn't look half bad," he admitted. "Lucky for you, Bailey, it looks like you heal quickly."

"Good. It's hard to baby an injury like that."

Ice carefully washed, cleaned and rebadged it.

By the time she was done, Bailey's expression was no longer quite so complacent. Instead it was slightly green. He knew how she felt. Gently they got Bailey back on her feet. With a smile of thanks to Ice, he led Bailey to the elevator and upstairs to her room.

When she walked in, she whispered, "Okay, now I'm so ready to lie down."

He quickly pulled back the bedding. "You need any help?"

She kicked off her shoes and whispered, "No thanks. I'm fine. Or I will be as soon as I'm horizontal again."

He stood at the doorway, uncertain if he should leave or stay. He let out his held breath when she carefully stretched out on the bed with a groan of relief.

She waved her hand, shooing him away. "I'll be fine."

"It's still early, so, if you wake up again, I'm right next door."

"I hope I sleep right through until morning. It'll likely take a bomb to wake me up otherwise." She closed her eyes and, right in front of him, fell asleep.

Chapter 10

THE SCREAMING NOISE ripped through her mind and into her dream. Only it wasn't a dream. Blasting her back to awareness, Bailey bolted to her feet and cried out in pain as her back wrenched, twisting her muscles in agony. But the high-pitched noise was worse. She clapped her hands over her ears and put her feet into the shoes left by her bed, rushing to pull open the door. All she wanted was for that noise to stop. Nobody was in the hall.

"Hello," she cried out. "What's going on?"

Dakota was supposedly next door to her room. She knocked on his door hard. The door swung open at her near-pounding, and she could see the larger room, masculine in its decor, was empty.

She made her way slowly down the corridor, the alarm driving hammers into her head. When she reached the elevator, she pushed the button to call the car to take her to the main floor.

As the door opened, several people rushed into the elevator beside her. She looked at them in surprise. "What's going on?" she cried out.

Dakota stepped in the elevator last. He stepped closer to her, saw her hands over her ears and wrapped an arm gently around her shoulders. Pulling away one of her hands, he whispered, "Security's been breached."

She stared at him in horror. "What do we do?"

"I was coming to you, but, now that you're here, I'm taking you to the control room."

She glanced around at the others. "What about them?"

"Everybody has a routine. We do this as a fire drill on a regular basis. So everybody knows exactly what to do."

The door opened but on a different floor than she'd been on before. Several people got out ahead of them. Dakota ushered her toward the door on the side and pounded in a weird tempo rap, and the door opened.

Ice stared at her, then smiled. "Come on in."

Bailey stepped inside, the door closing behind her, and instantly there was blessed silence. She dropped her hands and whispered, "Thank God."

Ice laughed. "Yes, it's loud but for a good reason." She motioned to a couple chairs on the far side. "Take a place over there and sit down. We're still tracking the intruder."

"Somebody's actually broken into the house?"

"Not the house. But someone's on the property."

And that's when Bailey realized the walls in this room were full of monitors. One huge bald-headed man, who introduced himself as Stone, sat at the computers with Merk. The two studied the feed covering all corners of the property.

"Stone, can you see anyone in your quadrant?" Ice asked as she walked over to stand behind the bald man.

Stone shook his head. "Not yet. I must get up there and take out some of those bushes. They're big enough to hide a man."

Bailey silently agreed.

Suddenly Merk called out, "There he is."

She wanted to lean forward to see, but the monitor was surrounded by enough people as they studied the intruder and his location.

"Okay, he's up on the northeast side," Ice said.

Levi's voice came through a loud speaker. "Heading there now."

And Bailey realized the compound had an intercom system. With them watching the intruder and Levi's progress, these people manning the control room could direct Levi and whoever else to where the intruder hid.

"Watch your six," Ice said. "We've only seen one, but that doesn't mean he came alone."

"Who's checking the road?" Levi asked.

"The new camera at the bend isn't operational. It's possible they've taken it out. We need to get someone out there to check on it."

"In that case, a vehicle is likely parked down there. We need somebody to look."

Merk stood up. "I've got that. I'll go through the tunnel. They won't see me from there. I'll check that bend easily enough." And just like that he was gone.

Ice took Merk's seat and typed on the keyboard.

Bailey was fascinated, terrified, hopeful and completely shocked that somebody would try to break into the compound. "Even if they got into the building, they have to know over a dozen people are in here."

"They know. They are looking for you, most likely."

"Sure, but how would they find me?"

"Chances are they wouldn't have to look too closely. I suspect he's carrying C-4 and is planning to blow up the entire compound anyway."

"They'd have blown up the compound?" she whispered. "For real?"

Stone chuckled. "Even so, C-4 would've been detected

before he got within twenty feet of the house. We have all kinds of sensors out there. Explosives are something we always keep track of."

She nodded, but inside she was numb. That these people talked about bombs—as in completely blowing up and annihilating a beautiful building like this one—in such a nonchalant manner was horrifying in itself. Something was wrong with the world that not only did people think that was justifiable but also that Ice and Stone considered it a normal everyday occurrence.

"You just want to see what happens if he makes it close enough to the house," Ice chided Stone.

He chuckled. "Of course I do. I put that one in there. Cost a fair bit of money too. But, so far, the external security system works well enough that we never get a sneaky bastard in that close to set off the new alarm."

Bailey listened, half dazed. This was so not the world she knew. And yet, at the same time, she was caught in the middle of it.

Another voice called into the panic room. "Does anybody want coffee?"

Alfred. The calm within the storm. The sanity within the chaos. The regular man doing the regular job to keep all the specialists running. Because, even in chaos, everybody still needed food and coffee.

She bolted to her feet. "I'll help Alfred."

Ice studied Bailey, took a careful look at her face and then nodded. "I'm letting you out. Before you come back in, you'll have to stand on the left-hand side of the door so I can see your face. I have a camera directed right there." She pointed so Bailey could see where she'd need to stand.

"I can do that."

Ice pressed the button, and a small *click* sounded as the double locks released on the door. Bailey opened it and stepped out.

From there she made her way back to the elevator and down to Alfred's kitchen. She walked into the large room and saw him setting up trays of coffee. "Let me help."

He glanced at her. "Sure. We've got men all over the place. And somehow, no matter what time of day or night, when things like this happen, coffee's always needed. When it's over, it'll be coffee laced with something else."

She took her cue from him and found her sense of balance by working at his side. "Does this happen often?"

He shook his head. "In the beginning, we had some drug cartels after Levi and Ice. Things got a little hairy then. But they have certainly beefed up their defenses and have built a fortress here now. We still run drills monthly. And every time a new security system is installed, we're given ample time to recognize where, when and how to deal with any breaches to it."

"Is this your world too?"

At her wording, he turned and looked at her. "All of Levi's recruits *were* military. But none of us are now. The women have all joined us one by one. We have one who's ex-military herself and, of course, so is Ice. She's a helicopter pilot, and those are her babies outside. That *was* our world. It is no longer. We created *this* world. It's a haven for all of us now. Even those without a military background." He smiled at her and added, "Like you."

She gave him a bright smile, picking up one of the two trays Alfred had prepared. "Where does this go?"

"If you know how to get back into the control room, then take that one up to Stone, Ice and Merk."

"Merk left. He headed out through the tunnel to look at the bend, thinking he could view any vehicle on the road because the camera on that side is no longer working."

Alfred raised an eyebrow. "Sounds like you're catching on real fast."

She laughed. "Not really but I'll be fine as long as I can get through this without losing my mind. I'll feel much better if I can be at least as calm as the other women."

"You're handling this like a pro."

She took the cups off the tray, but he added a couple muffins to it, so she replaced the cups.

"Take these too for Ice and Stone. They're both big eaters. And then, if you want, come back."

Armed with a mission she knew she could accomplish successfully, she headed off.

She stood in the correct position for Ice to see her and then knocked on the door. Ice let her in. She delivered the coffee and treats, then walked back out again. She headed to the kitchen to find Alfred must have left to deliver the other tray. But she had no idea where he had gone. She set about cleaning up the little bit of mess he'd made and then poured herself a cup of coffee. When Alfred didn't return, she got a little worried. She didn't know how their intercom worked, but, if Alfred had called them in the control room, there must be a way to make contact from the kitchen.

On one of the kitchen walls, she found a computer monitor system and what looked like speakers. She pressed one of the buttons and said, "This is Bailey. I'm looking for Alfred."

Her voice floated throughout the entire building, making her wince. She stepped back and waited.

Ice's voice was heard next. "When did you last see him?"

"After I delivered your coffee, I came back here. He had

prepped another tray, and I assume he's taken it, but I don't know where he went."

"Ten minutes ago?"

"About that."

"Give us a minute."

Bailey remembered all the monitors, how they could look at inside the house and outside at the property and presumed they were doing a full-on check of the interior of the building. No way an intruder should've made it this far in. But, while they were looking west, was anybody studying the east? Still the entrance gates were closed, so somebody must have gone over the gates or underground. … Like in the tunnel. She pushed the button and asked, "Any way to see inside the tunnel?"

Ice's voice turned brisk. "That's on the same camera that's now out of commission. I need you up here now."

Hearing the hard note in her tone, Bailey raced from the kitchen and headed for the elevator. It stood open. She stepped in and closed the doors, willing the elevator to move faster. She hit the third button to go upstairs. Just as she stepped back to wait, an arm wrapped around her neck and a hand slapped over her mouth.

Her strangled scream escaped but so low she knew no one could hear. She had no air left to scream with. She wanted to fight, yet she had no strength, and, no matter what movement she made, her back screamed in agony. But screaming with agony had to be a hell of a lot better than going down with whatever this asshole had in store for her. She chose the other option—to stand still. And wait for instructions.

When his voice, hoarse and raspy, whispered in her ear, she knew it was the worst possible outcome.

The man said, "Bitch, you'll get yours now."

DAKOTA QUICKLY MOVED around the outside of the building, checking for any intruder who may have made it through the external perimeter. They were short-staffed, but the remaining people at the compound had all taken appropriate roles as needed to man the security system parameters. His headset crackled.

"Merk went out the tunnel to check on the blind spot. The new camera is not working."

Dakota swiveled, looking in the direction of the bend at the corner of the road, an area they'd thought they'd addressed. But, if that camera was down, somebody helped bring it down. In which case …

He reached out and pushed the button on his comm. "Has Merk confirmed he made it outside?"

"No." Ice's voice shifted. "Can you check that out?"

He slipped around the building and raced up the hill toward where the tunnel exit was. Just as he reached a hilltop, he dropped to the ground and inched over to look below.

"A vehicle is at the opening. So far no sign of Merk." Dakota made his way down a few feet to a small outcropping. There he crept around to the front where the larger shrubbery was. The tunnel came out just beside it. He crept forward, and the moonlight exposed everything. "Footprints at the tunnel." As he studied them, his heart sank.

"Going which way?" Ice asked, her voice hard.

"The wrong way. You have an intruder in the house. I repeat, you have an intruder in the house. I'm coming in through the tunnel."

He took one last look at the truck below. He couldn't tell if somebody else waited down there as a getaway driver or if the intruder planned to take off in the vehicle once he did whatever he planned to do here. "The truck is still sitting there. No idea if we have a bogey inside. Going silent." He shut down his communication and slipped into the tunnel.

Small running lights ran alongside the tunnel, just enough that he could see ahead of him. The tunnel was clear. Moving as lightly as possible, he raced down the long passage. This opening was built well before they had moved into the compound. One of Levi's greatest finds was when he realized this little secret entrance to the property. But it also meant, if anybody else found it, it now became a weakness.

Dakota's heart pounded; Bailey was inside the house. And, knowing her, she hadn't stayed put either. He wanted to send a message to Ice but couldn't take the chance. He had to trust everybody was doing their jobs. But he could check. "Ice is Bailey okay?"

"No," Ice said her voice terse. "She was looking for Alfred, then ordered to return to the safe room given the camera issue but hasn't' arrived. I'm looking for her."

Shit.

He made it all the way through the tunnel without seeing signs of anyone. And that wasn't good. Just as he approached the tunnel entrance to the house, he found a crumpled body. Using his cell phone light, he checked, finding Merk, on his side, blood oozing from a head wound.

He clicked on his comm and whispered, "Merk's down. I repeat, Merk's down. Head injury needs medical attention stat. Six feet from house entrance inside tunnel."

He didn't wait for a response but turned off his comm as he slid up to the tunnel's entryway into the house. He unlatched the closures, sliding open one of the two doors just enough so he could search the area in front of the double doors. Two deliberately mounted mirrors were inside so, if each door was pushed open half an inch, one of the two mirrors would be in sight, giving a visual of the hall. It was empty. He slipped out.

Now where had the intruder gone?

On the main floor Dakota silently went to the right and checked the kitchen and dining room. Nobody was here, but someone had been. Trays of coffee—some full cups, some empty cups—sat on the counter. He did a quick sweep of the main floor living room, TV room, even the boardrooms down here. Over three thousand square feet in just one long section. And it was empty. That meant the asshole had gone upstairs.

He also didn't know how many intruders there were. Dakota took the nearest stairwell and did a quick search up it. Stairwell empty. Dashing downstairs again, he hit the elevator button. It took its time. As if it had come down from the upper floor. It was empty.

He headed back to the stairs and raced up to the second floor. There he slipped around the corner. This floor had a lot of the bedrooms. He could go through and search every room, but he had no way to know where everyone was without giving away his position to the asshole. What he needed was the alarm to give the alert that an intruder had made it inside and upstairs. He tapped his comm, issued the order.

Instantly a harsh rhythmic beat whipped through the house. He heard several of the bedrooms bolting shut from the inside. That was good. That meant some of their people, assigned as the backup team if needed, were locked in and safe. He raced down to his room, made a quick check. It was empty. Then he opened Bailey's room. Unfortunately her room was completely empty too.

While standing in her room surveying the hallway, he clicked on his comm and said, "Bailey is not in her bedroom. She's nowhere to be found."

Ice's voice came through clear. "I can see her. She's on the third floor, walking in view of our cameras. But she's not alone. Single gunman, assault rifle over the shoulder, two handguns, one at the back of her neck. Alfred is also missing. I repeat, Alfred is also missing."

Shit. When things went bad, they went bad in a big way. Somebody needed to get to Merk and find Alfred, but taking out the known gunman was priority one. Ice would be organizing the others to help. Dakota would make his way to the top floor before he did anything else.

Just as he stepped into the hall and around the corner, the elevator doors opened. Levi and Rhodes exited, both armed and ready, grim looks on their faces. Dakota gave them an update.

Levi nodded. "We've moved Merk into the medical clinic. Stone will stay with Ice in the control room. She's unarmed."

"The gunman and Bailey are upstairs, heading toward the offices or the control room."

"Some asshole has blueprints of this property," Rhodes said in a furious whisper. "That is something we need to fix."

Dakota nodded. Not that it would be easy. "Could have come from any number of places."

The three split up, taking three different ways upstairs. Dakota went straight to the roof. From the roof, he could climb down a fire escape on two sides. It would allow him to come around and enter Levi's bedroom, then proceed to the hallway. With any luck from there, he should see the gunman and Bailey.

He made it down the nearest fire escape, popped open the window and slipped into the bedroom. Crossing to the main doors, he slid open a small panel on the interior wall which gave him not only a view of the outside hallway but a clear space to shoot through.

And there was the gunman. He stood, looking around as if heading for a particular room. Dakota didn't waste a moment. As the gunman turned and shifted away from Bailey, Dakota fired. The shot slammed into the man's gunhand, and the pistol went flying. The gunman roared and went after his second gun. But Levi was on him.

Bailey, now free, raced to the far wall. She flattened herself just out of Dakota's sight. Dakota opened the bedroom door and jogged to her side. He planted himself in front of her and said, "Did you see a second man?"

She shook her head. "No. Only the one guy grabbed me in the elevator. I didn't see anyone else."

Levi had already cuffed the gunman's hands behind him. But the man was still bucking and fighting, twisting to get a good kick at Levi.

Dakota slammed his boot into the man's head. He crumpled, silent. The last thing they needed was him sending out any alerts to a second gunman.

Rhodes joined them, then stepped up to the control room door, where Ice could see his thumbs-up sign. Instantly the door opened.

She came out, took one look at the gunman on the ground, took one of the two weapons Rhodes held and said, "I have to get to the clinic."

Bailey looked at her. "Is someone hurt?"

Ice moved toward the elevator. As it opened, she called out, "Merk."

Dakota tried to stop her, but there was no stopping Bailey when she wanted to go. She raced ahead, just barely making it into the elevator before it closed.

He stared at the closed door. "Damn."

This was not exactly how he thought the evening would end.

Chapter 11

"I CAN HELP," Bailey said as she reached out to the side of the elevator for support.

Ice shot her a sideways look. "That statement would carry more conviction if you could stand on your own two feet." Her voice was calm.

"Just give me a moment," Bailey said with a half laugh. "I'm not used to being held at gunpoint."

"You may not be used to it, but you handled yourself well."

Bailey shook her head. "All I could think about was the number of times, when my husband was dying, that I had wished I could die instead. The number of times since his death where I had wished the fight would be over, and I could go join him. And then suddenly, a gun's at my head, and all I can think about is how much I want to live."

Ice turned to look at Bailey and smiled a breathtaking smile. "And that was the right decision. Because, even in death, those left behind have to grieve. But when you do accept there is a life for you again, and you understand you have to struggle, it doesn't matter what happens. The future is about having a chance at life, and it's worth it."

"For a moment, I could see my husband's face. That smile he had just before he passed away," Bailey admitted, feeling tears clogging her throat. "And I thought I would join him. And then there was this split second … like I was shifting through time, and I saw Dakota's face." She shook her head. "I'm sure he'd be laughing at that right now."

"Dakota would not laugh at that. He'd be honored."

"I don't even know him."

"You know what's important about him. You know he'd never leave an injured woman on the street. You know he'd never leave anyone unprotected and in need of assistance. You know he's honorable, has integrity, and would do anything to help anybody. It doesn't matter what other qualities he has when those are at the core. You can work with all the rest."

"I don't even know if he has a girlfriend," Bailey said quietly, in case anybody else was within hearing range.

They exited the elevator, walking down the hall toward the medical clinic. Bailey almost ran to keep up with Ice— her long legs ate up the miles.

In the medical clinic, Sienna and another woman stood at Merk's side. Sienna looked up with relief. "I can't find any other injuries. Looks like one blunt force trauma to the head."

Ice nodded. "It could be much worse," she announced.

"It could. This is bad enough though," the other woman said.

Ice reached over the table Merk lay on. "Katina, he will be fine. If anybody in this house has a hard head, it's Merk."

Sienna chuckled. "I would've said Rhodes deserved that award."

Bailey stood at the man's feet, her gaze studying his posture. "Did you check for breaks or anything else?"

Sienna nodded. "A quick search. Why? You see something?" She joined Bailey at the table.

"His knee looks off," Bailey said.

"Head trauma first. Knees later," Ice said.

She set about cleaning the wound, and Bailey watched in astonishment as Ice clipped and cut the hair back, checked the bones around the wound, telling Katina to grab the portable X-ray machine. Instantly a professional stainless steel–looking machine was wheeled over, and Ice took images. When she returned with a digital copy on the tablet in her hand, she said, "He has a concussion, but no bones were broken from that wound. We can deal with this."

She quickly set about stitching the wound closed. With that done, she turned and checked out the rest of him. "His blood pressure is fine. He'll have a nasty headache, and he'll be plenty pissed when he wakes up."

"If he wakes up," Katina said in a small voice.

Bailey understood how Katina felt. The number of times Bailey laid beside her husband when he was so ill, and she knew waking him up was for her sake, not his. It would have been so much kinder if he'd just closed his eyes, took his last breath and left this existence. But still all she wanted was for him to wake up.

Ice did a quick physical check of his knee. "It's puffy, as if he's fallen on it. We'll ice it, but there's good movement, no breaks that I can see from here. I'll go ahead and X-ray anyway."

Bailey realized how silly she was to think she could help. Ice had this more than in hand. And, with two other assistants, Ice didn't need Bailey. She slowly made her way to a set of chairs off to the side and sat down.

Ice glanced at her sharply. "Are you okay?"

"Just realized you don't actually need me here."

"It depends," Ice said. "The night's young. I've had as

many as four in here at a time. And then there aren't enough spare hands. I can't do everything all at once."

"And if it gets really ugly?"

Ice raised her head from studying Merk's knee and stared at Bailey. "If it's that bad, I warm up the chopper, and we fly to the hospital. Every one of these men and women who live in this house are under my care. I'll do my damnedest to make sure they get the best care that's available."

And Bailey believed Ice. This place was one hell of a unit. They were all so very blessed to have this home and each other. "Did anybody find Alfred?"

The two women looked at each other. Ice said, "I believe the men are searching for him now." She glanced over at the second bed. "Chances are he'll be here in a few minutes."

Bailey stood back up again and walked over to the double glass doors, stepping into the hallway. "Where's his room?"

Katina walked to her. "Let me show you." Katina led Bailey to one of the lower floors.

"Why would Alfred have his rooms down here?"

"He actually has an apartment here all to himself. It's not belowground on his side."

They walked up to an unassuming-looking door, and Katina rapped on it hard. There was no answer. She tried the handle and pushed it open. "Alfred, are you here?"

There was no answer.

Katina flicked on the light switch. They both did a quick search to make sure he wasn't lying injured somewhere.

Bailey noticed the glass doors on the opposite side, set into a rock wall. "Amazing. How did he end up with this?"

"The room itself was here before, actually built into the rock, but Levi and Ice finished it for him."

Bailey loved the natural beauty of the room, the light shining bright inside. She turned and headed back out. "We should tell Ice that he's not here."

"Absolutely. Let's do a quick tour down here to make sure he's not anywhere else."

With Katina once again leading the way, Bailey visited a massive fitness room, various storerooms, multiple cold rooms, and a myriad of empty rooms. The place seemed to go on forever.

"This place is huge!" she exclaimed when they opened another room that appeared to be a huge walk-in storeroom.

Katina nodded. "It is indeed." Up ahead was a large double freezer door with a lock on the outside. She pulled the key from the side, unlocked the door, and, with Bailey's help, they pulled them open to reveal a huge walk-in cooler. Thankfully no Alfred in there. With the doors closed once again, and the lock back in place, the two women retraced their steps to Ice.

At Ice's look, Katina shook her head. "No sign of him anywhere, and, yes, we checked inside the cooler."

"I'll take that as a good sign." Ice nodded. "The defense team hasn't found a second intruder yet. But they are on it. With Merk taken care of for the moment, I'll join the search for Alfred."

"Where else could he be?" Bailey asked.

"This place is massive. So in any one of the bedrooms, storage rooms, closets or offices." Ice shrugged. "We'll do a full-on search now." She motioned at Katina. "You sit and watch Merk."

Katina stepped up, held Merk's hand and whispered, "Always."

Ice dragged over a desk chair to the side of the bed.

"Here. Make yourself comfortable, and call me when he wakes up. I'll lock you in." She hit a sequence of numbers on the keypad inside the room.

This time Ice led the way out. Once again her long legs ate up the distance so Bailey had to run to keep up. And so did Sienna, which made Bailey feel somewhat better.

Instead of taking the elevator, Ice took the stairs, two at a time down to the first floor. There she started in the kitchen, checking the pantry, any space big enough to hide Alfred.

When she looked in the commercial dishwasher, Bailey's stomach sank. Was it really a viable option at this point? She hoped not. Because that would mean somebody had folded up the poor old man and stashed him away where he wouldn't be seen. Even worse would have been if the assholes had turned on the damn thing. Thankfully it contained dishes only.

But slightly unnerved, Bailey moved a little slower as she followed the women while they went systematically through the kitchen, dining room, the extra seating area with the small tables, the massive living room, checking behind all the nooks and crannies, and then they came to a set of mirrored double doors off the main entryway on the left-hand hallway.

Ice opened them up with a cry of surprise, and she caught Alfred as he tumbled to the floor.

Bailey ran to Alfred's side. She fell to her knees and then checked for a pulse. "He's alive."

Ice went into action, doing a full-body check.

Bailey stared at the space where they'd found him. It appeared to be a broom closet. Somehow Alfred must have been taken unawares. But not here. He wasn't delivering hot coffee and muffins to the first floor. He was attacked somewhere else and stowed away here. And where was his tray? She studied Alfred closer and found blood on his left temple, although not as much as had been on Merk's head. And Alfred had been propped up against the one door; the other door had then been shut on him. When both had been opened, he fell out.

Ice pressed something in her ear. That was the first time Bailey realized Ice had been in communication with the control room the whole time.

"We found Alfred. Also injured. Another head wound. Front closet," Ice said.

A weird static-crackle followed as somebody answered. When she was done, she stood and walked over to the front closet and looked to see if anything was different. Ice said, "I'm the last person who would actually know if anything was missing or had been added or changed in here." She shook her head.

Then the paneling on the opposite wall opened up, and Dakota came running through. He held a weapon in his hand, and a rifle was slung over his shoulder, hanging on his back.

Bailey straightened in surprise.

He came to a sudden halt, his gaze going to her and immediately dropping to Alfred, then back to her. "Are you hurt?" Dakota barked.

She shook her head mutely. Outside of having surprised her with his sudden appearance, she wasn't sure what to think of his fully weaponized garb in warrior mode. Her gaze drifted to the double doorway behind him. "I didn't even know those doors existed," she explained. "It just looks like the hallway paneling."

He nodded. "I was checking the tunnel again to make sure nobody had gone in after Levi brought Merk out."

"And Levi?" Ice asked.

"He should be downstairs any moment with his prisoner."

"Good," Ice snapped. "I want to talk with that man." She motioned at Alfred. "Can you?"

Dakota holstered his weapon, bent down and gently lifted Alfred, cradling him in his arms, heading to the medical clinic with Ice and Bailey and Sienna following.

As they all converged on the clinic, Katina's gaze widened when she saw Alfred. "Oh, my God! Is he hurt too?"

Dakota carefully laid the man down on the second bed and stepped out of the way. Sounds came from around the corner. He stepped back and nodded to Ice. "That's Levi."

In a no-nonsense voice, she stated, "I want that gunman conscious when I get there."

THANK HEAVENS BAILEY was okay.

It was hard to explain the sense of relief that washed through Dakota when he realized Bailey was safe. He had had so many close calls in his life that he knew, one of these days, somebody wouldn't make it. When he'd lifted Alfred, Dakota had had a second shock. The man was lightweight, nothing to him, despite his commanding air. Dakota didn't even know how old Alfred was. He'd always seemed so fit and capable, but he was slight of build, and, right now, with a head injury, he looked impossibly weak and old.

Dakota stepped back another few steps, leaving Alfred in Ice's capable hands, and followed the noise to where Levi had taken his prisoner.

The men, when not working paying jobs, were in the process of setting up a makeshift jail down here, not wanting to go through the structural work required to put in a full set of bars and a gate. But Dakota wasn't sure any other option would work. Honestly, they could probably do the work themselves because no way in hell would they get a permit for this, and they didn't want anybody to know they had something like that down here anyway.

The Internet made everything accessible for anyone who knew where to look.

Dakota walked over as Levi pulled off the man's shoe. The gunman was awake but secured, his legs clipped to the chair legs with special bindings; his hand-cuffed wrists duct-taped to the chairback. For added measure his neck had been duct-taped to the chairback as well.

Dakota stepped up behind Levi. "His face isn't familiar to me. I don't know who he is."

"Neither do we," Levi said. He quickly picked up a cell phone, took a picture and said, "Let's see if Detective Mannford does."

"It's not one of the usual henchmen, so I would presume he's hired muscle." Dakota studied the man, watching for a reaction. But all he got was a stone-cold glare. "Although he's a little too well weaponized for a henchman or hired muscle. He also had seen the blueprints for the property. Sounds like a pro."

"Isn't that the same thing the rest of you do?" Bailey asked.

Dakota glanced up and over at her and shook his head. "No. Not at all. We protect, serve and save. Mercenaries and assassins will do all kinds of things, from kidnapping to taking out powerful leaders. They often have a specific target as the job. They take them out and leave—and for a preset fee."

She shrugged. "Sounds the same to me."

"Not quite." But he had watched the intruder's face at her words. The man hadn't liked her comment at all.

"Yeah, he's a pro. Or he wants us to think he's a pro. He didn't like the idea of being called the same thing as a mercenary."

"Pros have professional pride," the intruder snapped. "Mercenaries just have a price tag."

"They are the same shits," Levi said, his voice hard.

"Not even close. One has ethics. The one takes on anything. There is a hierarchy in all professions."

Bailey snickered. "I'm pretty damn sure any pro's pride is a malleable thing, based on the paycheck."

In a move that surprised all of them, she walked up to the intruder, swung back and open-handedly slapped him across the face.

He glared at her.

"That's for hitting Alfred," she said. "You aren't a pro if you have to hurt an old man."

Although her actions had surprised him, Dakota was in full agreement, though he was pretty sure Alfred wouldn't like to be referred to as an old man.

Levi spoke to Bailey. "You may want to return to the medical clinic."

She faced him. "Are you going to kill him?"

Levi's eyebrows shot up, and he stared at her. "Do you care?"

She thought about it for a long moment and then said, "Can't say I really want that to happen, but, if he attacks anyone else, I'm okay with it. After what he did to Alfred and Merk, he certainly deserves the same back, but I don't want you to get in any trouble."

Levi's lips quirked. "Okay, then I won't kill him unless he attacks me."

"And, if he attacks Dakota, I'll kill him myself." She shot a warning look at the intruder, noting the surprised glint in his eyes. And she turned and left the room.

Dakota shook his head, a big grin on his face. "Wow, is it this place, this intruder or has Bailey always been like that?"

Chapter 12

BAILEY DIDN'T WANT to return to the medical clinic. She figured, now that some of the excitement was over, everyone would need food. She checked her watch—six o'clock—and it was, indeed, breakfast time or at least time for more coffee. Anything other than coffee would probably take an hour.

But Alfred shouldn't be cooking at all today. Possibly not for several days. She didn't want to step into his domain without permission, but it was the one thing she could do to help. Not knowing what she should cook, she walked upstairs to the kitchen and put on coffee.

She processed the kitchen contents to see if Alfred had plans for breakfast. An ample number of sausages and bacon were in the small freezer, but she couldn't find anything thawed out. She'd only been here one morning, so she didn't know if he put on a feast like that all the time or if it was just because of the extra people. The walk-in cooler was downstairs, but she wasn't sure she'd be up to taking food out and bringing it up.

Then she spied a second fridge. She opened it and, to her delight, found it full of fresh vegetables, fruits and several large briskets, waiting to be cooked. That she could handle, although that was probably for dinner.

As she slowly turned around in the kitchen, she struggled with what to prepare for breakfast. Sure, she could do fried eggs, but she didn't know how many people here liked them that way. She wished there was a simpler answer.

She frowned. Alfred wouldn't be short on the basics. In which case, she could make up a huge batch of cinnamon buns. She checked her watch again and calculated the time, realizing it would be tight. The dough had to rise at least once, although she'd learned a few tricks of the trade that would make the process faster. She searched the cupboards, wondering if she had all the ingredients available.

Very quickly she found what she needed. With the largest bowl she could find, and the island completely cleared off, she went to work. Rhodes arrived first, looking for coffee. He poured several cups and stared at her with curiosity but never said a word. He filled a tray with the coffee cups and disappeared.

She realized he'd almost emptied the coffee pot. She put on a second pot and continued with breakfast. She hadn't said anything to him, just gave him a small smile. She wasn't exactly sure if tripping into Alfred's domain was a big no-no or not. She worked as fast as she could, wanting to get the buns done before anybody else showed up.

It had been a while since she'd had to work at that pace, but she picked it up quickly again. Her hands easily fell into the same rhythm she needed to make massive loaves of dough.

As she worked, she hummed gently. She'd forgotten the joy of cooking. Somewhere along the line she'd forgotten the happiness of just being alive. If she learned one thing from all this mess, it was that she had to enjoy every day, not just the special days. There had been few—very few—special days in her world in a long time.

With the buns in the oven a short while later, she cleaned up and wiped off the counter and washed her dishes when she heard a sound behind her.

Alfred, leaning on Ice's arm, stood with stubborn pride in the kitchen doorway.

She rushed over. "How are you feeling? Are you sure you should be up?"

He patted her hand and gave her a small smile. "Of course I should be up. It was only a knock on the head."

She snorted. "A knock that can be very serious."

Ice led him to the small table in the kitchen and sat him down. Bailey picked up a coffee cup, filled it and brought it to him.

Ice spoke to Alfred, with a nod toward Bailey. "As far as I'm concerned, you have found your partner for the next few days. If need be, everyone here can wrestle food for themselves. I can cook in a pinch as well. I've done it before."

Alfred gave her a smile. "Go. Bailey and I have things to take care of. We'll figure it out."

Ice grabbed a cup of coffee and disappeared. He leaned over the tabletop and in a low voice asked, "All right, what kind of cinnamon buns did you make?"

She grinned. "Is it okay? I felt terrible, thinking I might be stepping on your toes."

He settled back with a weary sigh. "It's a damn relief, that's what it is."

"But they're all used to things like sausages and hash browns and pancakes. I just wasn't sure if this would be welcomed or not. It has sugar."

"It'll be refreshing. Every one of them has a damn sweet tooth. They will survive. If you made enough." He rolled his head toward her, a question in his eyes.

She winced. "I quadrupled what I would normally make. Honestly, some of the men here are big."

That startled a chuckle out of them both. "This bunch is definitely full of healthy eaters, and half of them aren't even here, off doing missions."

The aroma caught her nose. She lifted her nose and sniffed the air, got up and walked to the oven. Finding oven mitts hanging on the hook above the stove, she opened the first of three counter-height ovens and rotated each of the baking sheets containing the cinnamon buns.

When that was done, she sat back down again and said, "Maybe ten minutes."

"Perfect. You're on top of everything."

"I can make icing."

"Oh, lovely. I do that myself."

Then they embarked on a discussion of cinnamon bun bread and fast-rising yeast and other tricks of the trade.

A few minutes later she said with a happy sigh, "I forgot how much fun it is to cook."

He shook his head. "Now that is sad, because you're obviously very talented."

She snorted. "Hmm. You haven't tasted anything I've made yet."

He chuckled. "You stepped into a foreign kitchen, picked up the slack when needed, found ingredients you wanted and created something. That takes talent. It also takes a can-do attitude. And even better the kitchen is clean. So you also know how to function and clean up behind yourself and leave a place the way you found it."

Just then Dakota walked in. His nose wrinkled as if sniffing the air. His gaze zeroed in on Alfred. "I'm glad to hear you weren't badly injured, Alfred."

"He took a knock on the head and was unconscious. He should be in his apartment resting," Bailey said with a touch of exasperation. "But he won't listen."

Dakota nodded. "Like the rest of us, he has too much stubbornness for his own good." He cocked his head to the side, raised an eyebrow and said to Bailey, "You should easily relate."

Smiling, Alfred settled back. "We'll see how you feel when there's no food."

"I can scramble up seven dozen eggs, if need be," Dakota said. "I can't guarantee how they'll taste though."

Alfred smiled. "I'm sure they will all be fine."

Dakota studied him for a long moment. "How long have you been here?"

Alfred told him, "Just a few minutes."

Dakota's gaze zeroed in on Bailey. "Did you make whatever's in the oven then?"

She slunk a little lower in her chair. "Maybe."

He waggled an eyebrow. "What is it?"

She watched as he turned into a little boy right in front of her eyes. "What do you care? You can scramble seven dozen eggs," she teased.

"If that's something sweet," he said, almost dancing with hope, "every one of us will go down on our knees and thank you."

She shook her head. "I doubt it."

Alfred patted her hand. "Time's up."

She hopped to her feet, grabbed the oven mitts and opened the first oven door. She took out the first of four trays of golden brown cinnamon buns that had risen well over the top of the pan, the brown sugar bubbling atop each bun.

Dakota's whistle swept through the kitchen. Right behind him Rhodes and Levi stepped into the room. Their gazes were on the cinnamon buns in her hand.

She put the hot pan on one of the wire racks on the counter, pulling out the second tray and the third also. She retrieved the fourth cookie sheet and quickly flipped it upside down on a sheet of parchment paper. They looked at her in outrage.

"Why would you do that?"

She smiled and said, "You'll see." With the men watching, she wiped a wet dishcloth over the bottom of the pan. When she lifted the pan, it came off easily. As they watched, she took a spatula, scraped out the syrup the buns had been sitting in so it all flowed over the buns. "These are different."

She put the pan in the sink to soak. Turning to Alfred, she said, "Do you have any cream cheese?"

He motioned to the fridge closest to him. "In the bottom drawer."

She opened the big door, pulled out the drawer, found a huge block of cream cheese. Frowning, she grabbed a knife and hacked the cream cheese block in half. She tossed it into a mixer, added the rest of the icing ingredients while the men salivated beside her, impatiently waiting. She quickly slathered the top of the cinnamon buns with the cream cheese icing. When the icing melted and ran in front of them, their anticipation was palpable.

She didn't put any on the upside-down pastries.

Dakota pointed to them and asked, "What's with those?"

She just raised an eyebrow and stared at him. "What about those?"

He narrowed his gaze at her. "I want one of each." He

quickly added, "Please."

She dished up three plates for the three men. She gave Dakota one of each, an iced cinnamon bun and a sticky bun, yet put just one cinnamon bun on each of the other two plates.

Rhodes stared at her. "I know you love the guy, but surely he doesn't get that much special treatment."

Blushing furiously, she scooped up one of the upside-down buns for his plate too. Levi looked at her, and she chose the biggest she could find for him.

He grinned. "She already knows who's the boss."

"You shouldn't be eating them now. They're too hot."

After a snort from Dakota, the guys moved to the dining room, but there was only silence at first, followed by moans. She turned toward Alfred, grinning wildly. "May I get you one?"

He motioned to the upside-down sticky buns. "Only a half."

She took one of the sticky buns, cut it in half, slit it open, spread cream cheese icing on the open cut and sat down at the small table to share it with Alfred. Listening to the three men gorge on the cinnamon buns, the two of them sat in complete silence.

When he was done, Alfred whispered, "The best I've ever had."

Inside a smile unfurled, and she was sure it was the first time since her husband had died.

DAKOTA CLOSED HIS eyes and inhaled the cinnamon buns aroma. He would never say anything to upset Alfred, but, swear to God, this was the best damn cinnamon bun Dakota had ever had. He wasn't too sure what to do with the upside-down one, but he was game. As soon as he tasted the sugary flavored syrup all the way through the inside of the bun, he was hooked. He didn't slow down until both were gone. He stared at his empty plate and glanced over at Rhodes and Levi. Both were staring at empty plates.

Rhodes lifted his eyebrow. "Any chance of seconds?"

Dakota wasn't sure why Rhodes asked him, but, since Bailey had made them, Dakota might be the best bet to getting more. "I guess we'll have to find out," he said with a grin. He grabbed his plate, walked back into the kitchen to see Alfred and Bailey enjoying a cup of tea together. He held out his empty plate and, in his best Oliver Twist imitation, said, "Please, ma'am, may I have some more?"

Her face lit up.

He grinned. "They're delicious."

She hopped to her feet, saying, "You're just looking for a sugar fix."

But she cheerfully plated another cinnamon bun for him. He stood and waited. She looked at him and said, "You can't possibly eat a fourth, can you?"

Smirking, she gave him one of the upside-down ones, and he quickly disappeared into the dining room.

He had to make his way past Rhodes and Levi, both standing with their plates out. He could hear her laughter in the kitchen as she served them. He hadn't a clue she could cook like this, but she'd certainly found a way into everyone's hearts. The fact that Alfred was hurt, and likely shouldn't be in the kitchen at all, made her arrival all that much more perfect.

He refilled all three mugs of coffee, and the men sat down again. "I presume the intruder is in our jail?"

Levi nodded. "He is. But we don't have any ID. He's got nothing on him. Will you move his vehicle into the garage when you're done eating?"

"Will do. See if that will tell us anything."

"If we weren't so short on men, we'd be out there right now. Everybody's off on jobs. It's left us a little defenseless at home." Levi shook his head.

"But how can you tell how many we'll need when you don't know when you'll be under attack?"

Just then they heard a vehicle on the rocky driveway. Dakota bolted to his feet. "Who's driving the truck from the bend?"

"That would be Stone," Levi said with a smile, as he got a message over his comm. "He left the control room."

Bailey said from the doorway, "In the capable hands of Ice. She brought Alfred here and then headed back up."

Just then Stone walked into the kitchen and froze. His nose lifted, and he took one look at the cinnamon buns fast disappearing down his buddies' throats, and his gaze zeroed in on Bailey. "Is that cinnamon buns?" he asked hopefully. "You didn't let them eat them all, did ya?"

"No, there are lots left. I promise."

Stone nodded agreeably. "Good. Could I possibly have a couple?"

She disappeared into the kitchen while Stone sat down beside Levi. "I checked the glove box. No ID, no insurance, no registration papers."

"Of course. What if the license plates were stolen too?"

"Probably were. The VIN's been scraped off."

"That fits. We decided he was a pro. Now it's a matter of who could afford his wages."

"The mayor has that kind of money," Dakota said.

Just then Bailey delivered a large plate with four cinnamon buns from the kitchen and placed them in front of Stone. He took one look, and his smile was so bright it lit up the room. "Do I get double because of my size?" he asked. "Or have these pigs already eaten this much?"

She gave him a gentle smile. "Your size has nothing to do with it. If you need more, you tell me. They're already on seconds."

He glared at the men. "You would've finished all of them without even telling me they were here, wouldn't you?"

Levi snorted. "As you would have too, if you'd been here first." He looked at Stone's plate. "That's your first serving. We only got half that, so quit your complaining."

Bailey smiled and disappeared into the kitchen.

Stone lowered his voice. "What's with the upside-down one? Did she drop it?"

Dakota snickered. "You should try those first."

Stone gave him a look of disbelief. "She meant to put it upside down?" He picked it up and took his first bite. And then he stopped, a look of complete rapture on his face.

Dakota realized just how true that adage was. The way to a man's heart *was* through his stomach. Still his heart had already been awakened and on alert status when it met Bailey. But to know she could cook like this … Talk about being a keeper.

He almost choked at the word. If ever something meant *forever, marriage* and *permanency*, it was that word. Not so much related to this group, but he knew Mason, another SEAL at the Coronado base. Mason's Keepers group was legendary. And of course Legendary was Levi's group's name. Levi didn't ever want to hear the word *heroes* used in conjunction with his group, yet there was no doubt about it;

the women had coined multiple hero phrases as they had all joined the group. However, Levi probably liked those better than the matchmaking jokes.

Dakota wasn't sure what Bailey would think about all that yet. Or if she was even interested. He had to question why he was thinking about it. He was interested in her, but he knew she was still hurting from the loss of her husband. Not to mention she was a woman in need. And he'd never leave anyone in need if he could give assistance.

"Next move?" he asked Levi.

Levi laid down his fork, finished his last mouthful, then said, "Mannford will be here soon. He'll pick up the prisoner and take him to town."

Dakota nodded. "I know I'm from California and new here, but this is Texas. Any reason we can't just take him up the hill and shoot him?"

Levi gave a bark of laughter. "I keep forgetting how bloodthirsty you are. If we'd done so at the time, the attack would've been completely justified, but we needed information from him."

"We could just beat it out of him," Bailey said with a dark undertone from the doorway. She eyed Stone's plate, checking on his progress. But, since he still had one and a half left, she seemed content to leave him to finish it. "We're allowed to protect our property in any way, shape or means."

"That's correct, but torture is still not an allowable method of defense," Levi said gently.

Her shoulders dropped. "Right." She turned and walked back into the kitchen.

Dakota smiled. "She's been through a lot these last couple days."

"She's a trooper," Stone said, although his words were

hard to hear through the cinnamon bun in his mouth. He picked up the last bun and ate it in a few bites, setting his empty plate off to the side. "She's not only a trooper but she can cook. Nice choice, Dakota."

He shook his head. "It wasn't a choice."

Stone nodded sagely. "Isn't that the truth? When we get hit, we get hit, and we can do absolutely nothing about it."

"Hey, that's not what I meant either," Dakota protested. But the other men weren't listening.

"Do we trust Mannford?" Rhodes asked.

"We have to trust somebody. He is the detective on the case. And he comes highly recommended by Logan's father."

"Gunner? Maybe he could help out Bailey."

Levi shrugged. "He's been traveling lately, so I haven't brought him in on it. Not even sure he's home."

"What about the other new recruits?" Dakota asked. "We're shorthanded anyway. Don't you have other men you can bring in?"

Levi propped his elbows on the table. "I've spoken to Michael several times, but, so far, he's turned me down."

"Michael?" Dakota asked. "Do I know him?"

Rhodes piped up. "Michael Hampton. He did his time—left on a very sour note. Hell of a man, hell of a warrior. But his attitude toward the military brass took a hit."

Dakota snorted. "It did for a lot of us."

"Indeed. Now he's resting while he decides what he wants to do with his life. He lives a couple hours from here in a small town in Texas. But nothing is keeping him there. We keep coaxing him to move here."

"Give him time. It might work out."

"Maybe. But Michael is like a wall of granite that refuses

to move when he doesn't want to. You"—Levi pointed at Dakota—"would just want to push him along. As for other recruits, there are a few," Levi said slowly. "We just vetted two more. I'm not sure I have enough work to keep everybody going."

"And yet look at us," Rhodes said.

Stone nodded. "The world is in a rough place right now. That's why we're so busy."

A horn honked outside. They turned to the security screen to see a sedan sitting on the other side of the locked gate. Stone got up, walked over to the control panel and called out, "Identify yourself." As they waited, the monitor revealed the face of the man in the car.

"Detective Mannford."

"You're early."

"I am? Or I'm late. I haven't been to bed yet."

Stone hit the buzzer to unlock the gate. It swung wide.

It was a sign of how tired Dakota was that he hadn't even noticed the sound of the gate closing behind Stone as he drove the gunman's vehicle inside the compound earlier. They had several remotes they could take out with them if they needed to come back in on their own. It was a good system. Until people lost remotes, which happened a little too often to make everybody happy.

Mannford drove to the back door and parked. Stone walked over, opened the door and said, "You are just in time for coffee and a cinnamon bun."

"I won't say no," the man said, fatigue coloring his voice. "I don't mind telling you, it's been a pretty rough night."

"What's happened?"

Mannford stopped in the middle the room and looked at

Levi. "The mayor's been shot."

Chapter 13

"**W**HAT DID YOU say?" Bailey asked from the doorway. She shook her head, seeing the detective and the exhaustion riding his shoulders. "Did you actually say the mayor's been shot?" She slowly sank into the closest chair. "But I thought he was the one behind the attacks on me."

"It doesn't mean he isn't the one responsible for that," Levi clarified. "All we know right now is he walked out his front door and was shot. It went high, through his shoulder. He's expected to come out of this just fine."

Dakota piped up. "Cover up?"

Mannford looked over at him and frowned.

"Meaning, it was a deliberate attempt to make it look like he *wasn't* guilty? A bullet wound to the shoulder *is* fairly minor."

"It's possible." Mannford sat down at the long table beside Stone, accepting a cup of coffee. "But it's too early to tell."

"That is an extreme measure," Levi said.

Mannford nodded. "It certainly adds another twist to this tale." His gaze went from face to face, then over to Bailey. "Anybody here seriously injured?"

"Two," she snapped. "Merk is downstairs in the medical clinic with a head wound, and Alfred is awake and walking, but he was knocked unconscious and stuffed in the closet."

Alfred spoke up from behind them. "And I'm fine. I'll just take it easy today. Then I'll be right as rain tomorrow."

She shook her head. "You need at least a couple days off. Not walking around, no sudden standing up, in case you get dizzy." Her voice was bossy, like a nursemaid, but then she had had lots of practice in the role, and she did keep her voice soft, gentle. She turned back to Mannford. "Would you like a cinnamon bun?"

He smiled at her. "Thank you. That would be lovely."

She didn't know what kind of an eater he was so chose one of the normal cinnamon buns as she had twice as many of them and carried it out. Her gaze dropped to Stone's plate. "You actually ate them all?"

Stone protested. "They were good." He gave her a crafty smile. "I only had one serving. Do I get seconds?"

She raised her eyebrow. "You still want more cinnamon buns?"

He shrugged his massive shoulders and grinned. "I'm a big guy."

She returned, but instead of serving Stone, she had put a half dozen cinnamon buns onto a platter and put it in the middle of the table for all the men to help themselves.

As she walked back in kitchen, Alfred whispered, "Turn around."

She turned toward the dining room to see the platter she had just delivered was completely empty. Her jaw dropped. Her gaze went from one to the other of the men and not one of them looked guilty. Instead they had great big fat smiles on their faces. She turned back to Alfred. "How do you do it?"

He chuckled. "Practice."

"Will this be enough for breakfast or do we need to cook

something else?"

He looked at his watch. "The ladies will determine that. Considering how little sleep most people here got last night, chances are this will do, and then we'll set up for an early lunch."

"What'll we do for that meal?"

He said, "I'd planned on big subs."

"With French bread?"

He nodded. "Are you up for making some of those? I can sit here and do some slicing."

She peered around the corner. "What are we going to do, one loaf per male?" she asked sarcastically.

He chuckled. "You know? That's not a bad idea. That gives each of them three-quarters and their lady friends the remaining one-quarter."

"It's too early to get started, but I could do the prep now if you want."

He shook his head, patted her hand and said, "No. You go lie down for a few hours, then come back here. I noticed you're moving so much easier, and I'm really happy to see that. Let's not set you back."

She stopped and looked down at him in surprise. "I forgot all about my stitches."

"When we're busy, we tend to do that." He slowly straightened. "And I'll take my own advice and head to my room and see if I can't sleep for a few hours." Moving slowly but steadily he left the kitchen.

Bailey joined Dakota and sat down beside him. In a low voice she asked, "Should Alfred be left alone?"

Levi heard her. "We'll check on him in an hour or so."

She smiled. "In that case I'll grab a couple hours sleep too." She stood up and headed to her room.

With any luck, Mannford would leave with the intruder in cuffs. Then life here could get back to normal.

Whatever *normal* meant for her now. Still she was happy to leave the rest of the morning to the experts.

She made it to her room, very gently lay atop her comforter on her bed and closed her eyes. She was out almost instantly.

BACK IN THE dining room, Levi asked Dakota, "How's her back?"

"I think she's used to living with a lot of pain, and she just pushes through it," he said. "I have noticed her stiff movements, sudden winces. But, for the most part, it's almost as if she doesn't fully register the pain."

Levi nodded. "I did notice."

"Maybe it's a good thing," Stone said quietly. "We would all prefer somebody stoic and reserved, willing to help out when there is a need, than somebody who'll bemoan their injuries and expect to be looked after."

"She's certainly been an easy houseguest," Rhodes said.

"She's very lucky she found you guys," Detective Mannford said. "If she made those cinnamon buns, she's also a hell of a cook." He studied the plate, looked toward the kitchen and asked, "She's not married, is she?"

His tone was just enough that Dakota stared at him sharply. Mannford was in his mid- to late thirties, probably the strong, steady type she preferred. In a way Mannford would be like the husband she lost. The two might be a better match.

Instantly his mind said, *Better match than who?* And of course he already knew the answer to that question. And just as quickly came the thought, *No way was Mannford a better match*. Maybe he knew from watching his friends all pair up so quickly, like magnets coming together. As far as he was concerned, Bailey was his. But he wasn't sure she was ready for a relationship. Although her husband had died a while ago, some people took a long time to get over a loss like that.

"Shall we collect your prisoner then?" Levi asked.

Mannford said, "Yes. Although, if you don't mind, I'll sit here and have another cup of coffee and another cinnamon bun." He eyed the last one still on Stone's plate. "Unless you need that?"

Stone shook his head and slid it toward him. "I'll go grab the prisoner."

Dakota and Stone walked downstairs, where the intruder still sat, tied up in a chair. They released the ties around his wrists and neck, helped him out of the special clips binding his legs and helped him to stand. Then, with one grabbing each of his arms, they walked him upstairs to Mannford.

The detective took one look and nodded. He pulled his handcuffs from his back pocket and placed them on the table. Stone removed the handcuffs from the gunman to replace them with Mannford's and clipped them on the prisoner, sat him down, waiting until Mannford was done eating his cinnamon bun.

Finally, with an air of resignation and fatigue, the detective got up and walked outside to his car.

Dakota and Stone walked the prisoner ahead of them. Mannford's car had a caged divider between him and the prisoner, which Dakota was glad to see. Not all of the official vehicles did. They pushed the prisoner into the backseat of the car and locked the ankle brackets around the bottom of his legs and snapped the seat buckle around him. They stood in place and watched as Mannford drove away.

Stone clicked on his comm and said, "Ice, Mannford just left. Keep an eye on them for as long as you can."

Dakota watched and waited. "Doesn't it strike you as odd that Mannford didn't test the security bindings on his prisoner?"

Stone looked at Dakota. "Why should he? He trusts us."

"It isn't a case of trusting us." Dakota hated the doubts filtering through his brain. But something was just wrong about this, and it nagged at him. "Has Mannford been here before?"

Stone nodded. "Several times."

"Does he know about the tunnel?"

Stone turned and looked at him sideways. "Do you think he's involved?"

"If it was Lissa upstairs with stitches in her back from the first of two gunmen attacks, wouldn't you be looking at everyone?"

Stone frowned and glanced at the roadway. He turned back around and said, "Yes, I would." Stone walked inside. "I'll take a deeper peek at his background, see if there is anything suspicious."

"Don't bother. Ice already did," Dakota said. "We also need an ID for his prisoner," Dakota said.

Stone chuckled. "Got that. He's on the FBI's most wanted list. An assassin. Mostly working with the local drug lords."

"Figures." Dakota asked. "Still doesn't make him a local ..."

"Lots of hired guns move around the world from job to job. This guy's no different. But he's just done his last job here."

"We know for sure he came alone, right?"

"We sure don't," Stone said. "But we couldn't find any evidence of a second man around the buildings and no second man in the vehicle."

Dakota nodded. "I hear you, but my instincts aren't happy."

Stone spun and looked at him with a hard glance.

Dakota stared back quietly. "Are your instincts seriously telling you things are fine?"

Stone crossed his arms over his chest and studied Dakota for a long moment. "It's not saying things are fine. But no alarm bells are ringing."

Dakota brushed past him. "Good. Because mine are. Whenever yours start to sing, let me know. I don't believe this is over by a long shot."

Chapter 14

A WAKE A FEW hours later, Bailey didn't know if she should try for a shower. She was pretty sure Ice wouldn't approve of it. Only her back was itchy, blood-stained and sore. She reached around, managed to rip off the bandage, twisting so she could inspect the inflamed flesh. It surprised her to see how well it looked. She knew in theory she was supposed to keep her stitches dry, but how the hell did that work? On impulse, she turned on the shower. When it was warm, she stepped in under the spray. And moaned in joy, immediately feeling better.

The hot water slid down her face to her skin. Her head was grungy and was desperately in need of a good shampoo. She glanced around, delighted to see several hair care bottles beside her. Moving slowly, she gently shampooed her hair several times. She knew she was soaking her stitches, and that was probably not a good thing, but she was past caring about that in her overriding need to get clean. By the time she was done, she felt brave enough to face everyone's wrath for her actions.

She shut off the water, opened the shower and grabbed a towel. She dried off everywhere as best she could, then wrapped the towel tight around her to absorb as much of the water from her back as she could. By the time she made her way into the bedroom, she was feeling better but also tired.

She would need a new dressing, and she didn't have Ice's phone number to call her.

She put on a second borrowed T-shirt. Just as she finished dressing and hung up the towel, she heard a knock on her door. She opened it to find Dakota leaning against the doorjamb, his arms across his chest.

His eyebrows shot up when he noticed the wet hair. "You took a shower?"

She nodded. "Please don't be mad. I was just so grungy and needed to get clean."

He frowned. "Not sure what that means for your stitches."

"I was hoping Ice would put on a fresh bandage and tell me *no harm done.*"

"Then we better see what she says." He waited for her to step out and to close the door behind her. At the elevator he asked, "Did you get some sleep?"

She nodded. "I didn't think I would," she confessed. "Once I lay down and realized just how sore I was, all the lights went out."

"To be expected. You ended up doing a lot yesterday."

He walked into the dining area. She headed right for the fresh pot of coffee that had just finished dripping and poured herself a cup. Turning around she saw Ice and Dakota talking in the doorway. Ice took one look at her, nodded and then crooked her finger at her.

Taking her coffee with her, Bailey obediently followed Ice downstairs to the medical clinic. There she carefully lifted her shirt.

Ice took her time examining Bailey's back and put fresh antibiotic cream and a dry bandage on her. "I can understand you wanted a shower. Good thing it's healing nicely.

You didn't cause any more damage. The next time ask me, and I'll remove the bandage so you don't have to tear it off. Your skin is red now."

Bailey sat back up with a smile. "Thank you. Before I showered, I wished I had your number so I could've called you and asked."

Ice pulled out her phone, brought up her contact information and held it out for her. Bailey accepted it with a smile, as she grabbed her phone and added Ice's info to her Contacts. "Thank you." Together they walked back up to the kitchen. "Did the detective take the prisoner?"

Ice nodded. "He did, indeed. But I haven't connected with him since he left. I know he was exhausted, so I imagine he's asleep. As soon as I get an update from him, we'll take the next step."

"And that is?"

"Figuring out who shot the mayor."

Bailey gasped. "I actually forgot about that."

"I didn't," Ice said, her tone grim. "It's hard to know what that was all about, but it's got to be connected. So we need to get to the bottom of this."

"Isn't that the detective's job?"

She nodded. "Except they are pretty shorthanded, and it connects to our case. Although the police will be handling it, that doesn't mean we can't keep our own eyes and ears to the ground."

"And is that a worst-case scenario for me, or does it actually improve my case?"

"Too early to tell. But a second shooting is not a good thing."

"Right, somebody has to be getting desperate. It would make sense if it was the mayor's right-hand man who shot the mayor."

"It would make sense, but that doesn't make it the answer."

Ice headed to the dining room while Bailey went into the kitchen. She was delighted to find Alfred up. "Are you sure you should be in here?" she asked, not able to stop herself. "I can do lunch or whatever meal we're heading into," she joked.

Alfred shook his head. "It would be the sub sandwiches. If we prep everything, they can make their own." He motioned at trays full of sandwich fixings. "But maybe you could carry that to the table or get one of the men to."

"I'll take them," Dakota said as he stepped from the doorway where he'd apparently been standing. "She's pretty exhausted from doing too much last night."

Bailey turned to glare at him. "You didn't have to tell him that. I don't want him feeling guilty."

Alfred chuckled. "I don't feel guilty. It is what it is. She's feeling better now, and so am I."

"You didn't get enough sleep to feel better," Dakota said to Alfred.

Bailey smiled. "Nice to know you're so close you can tease each other like that."

Alfred smiled and patted her shoulder. "That's what family is all about. We take each other to task. It's either we overdo it or don't do enough. The rest of the time we just tease. But it's always done in good spirits and with a good heart."

Seeing him slicing cheese, she said, "Why don't I do that while you see about the next thing on your list?"

He handed her the cheese slicer. She quickly sliced a plateful of cheese slices. She turned in time to see Alfred pulling fresh loaves from the oven. She chuckled. "You do spoil them."

"I did feel bad about not making breakfast."

The oven had been turned off already. The buns had been sitting inside to stay warm. She put them on a rack for a few extra minutes of cooling while he finished preparations for everything else. When it was all ready, she loaded the large trays on a rolling cart and wheeled them into the dining room. Then they all sat down to eat.

Ice was late coming in with a grim look on her face. She sat down at the table. "I just spoke to Mannford. The prisoner was delivered successfully. Everyone is now currently looking for the shooter Bailey identified. His name is actually Jim Haskell."

"They should pick him up fairly quickly then," Levi said.

Ice shook her head. "I don't think so."

"Why not?" Bailey asked. "There can't be too many places in the city for him to run. It's one thing for him to shoot one person, but he also shot me, and then the mayor."

"*If* he shot the mayor. He's definitely guilty of the first two, but we can't guarantee he did that last one."

"It makes sense though," Dakota said. "He'd be covering his tracks. Maybe the mayor got nervous or tried to blame him. All you have to do is take care of the mayor, and nobody would be around to say otherwise."

Ice turned to look at him. "Except for Bailey."

Dakota lowered his sandwich and stared at Bailey. "She needs to stay here for the next week at least."

Bailey shook her head. "I have a job. I used to have a place to live. I need some clothes. Besides, I can't spend my life running from him. He could even leave the country."

"It's all too possible that he would do that." Dakota

shook his head. "But it doesn't matter. Until he's caught, you're not safe."

"You really think more people are involved?" she asked curiously.

He shrugged. "No way to tell but we do know an active shooter is out there. We had the intruder in here—an intruder, by the way, who says he was not hired by the mayor although when questioned he wasn't sure who paid the final bill."

Levi turned to look at Ice. "But then he would say that, wouldn't he?"

Ice shrugged. "Potentially he could also have been hired by the mayor's henchman, not the mayor himself."

Levi nodded. "It's all semantics to the killer. As long as he gets paid."

"Well, hopefully they will pick him up today so I can go back to my apartment."

"And do what? How many days off do you have?"

"This week, then it's back to work."

"Good. That means you stay here for the week."

She scrunched up her face, opening her mouth to refuse.

He lowered his voice. "And help out Alfred for a few days."

Her mouth closed as she considered it, and then she nodded. "As long as he doesn't object."

"It doesn't matter if he objects or not," Levi said, his voice hard. "He needs the help right now."

She snorted. "It doesn't matter what you say, it'll be Alfred who determines what help he needs."

Alfred gave her a glimmer of a smile. "Make sure it's what you want."

She rolled her eyes at him. "It's not exactly a hardship to

help."

But she knew it wouldn't be that hard to get him to agree. Alfred really was a sweet man. And he could use her help.

As soon as lunch was over and the kitchen cleaned up, she asked Alfred, "Did you eat a sandwich?"

He shook his head. "No, I'm not terribly hungry. I was planning on just having another half of a cinnamon bun."

At the counter she took the only cinnamon bun left and placed it in front of him. "You should have said something sooner. I would have saved you more. Once I brought them out, they disappeared quickly."

He chuckled. "All food does."

She studied his features, seeing the pale look on his face. "You're still not feeling well. You sure you don't want me to make dinner?"

He glanced at her. "You're just as injured as I am, even more so."

"But I'm several days into the healing, and Ice said my stitches look good." She frowned at the fridge. "I think I saw a couple briskets in there. Was that for dinner?"

"Yes, to roast them, serve them with horseradish."

They fell into a discussion of recipes and timing. She said, "Why don't you sit here? I'll get up and prep them, put them into the oven because we want a slow and long cook."

And that was what she did. By the time he was done with the last cinnamon bun, she had the briskets already in the oven, with him directing her where to find the equipment she needed.

By the time she had the kitchen cleaned, she felt a little on the weak side herself. Determined, she straightened up and said, "Now to see if I can persuade Dakota to take me shopping so I can get some clothes. But that's only if you agree to go lie down. Everything's prepped and ready until about an hour before dinner."

He smiled and said, "Deal."

And that was what they did.

She tracked Dakota down in the office. She stood hesitantly at the doorway, having never seen this space before. Sienna had her own desk; Ice and Levi were there with another half dozen desks in the large room. Dakota sat at one. She walked over to him.

He looked up in surprise, but a smile broke across his face. "What's up?"

"I was wondering if I could borrow a vehicle and go shopping."

"No way."

"I need clothes. Remember my apartment? Nothing was salvageable."

He glanced at his watch. "We'll go shopping. If you'll be ready in about ten minutes, I should have this done by then."

In her bedroom, she grabbed her purse off the table. She quickly checked her account to see if she had money and how much she had to spare. Which wasn't much, considering she had no idea what her expenses would be going forward. By the time she made it back downstairs wearing Sienna's T-shirt, Dakota waited in the foyer for her. He led her out and helped her into the small truck. She asked, "Why this truck?"

"It's cheaper on gas, and we aren't picking up anything large enough to warrant one of the bigger ones."

She chuckled. "Makes sense."

In the nearby little town of Wildon, they went to several

stores where she picked up a couple T-shirts, a pair of leggings and a pair of yoga pants for around the house. At another store she bought underwear. She stared down at her feet. "Wish I could've saved some of my shoes." She glanced at him. "You think we could go back and take another look?"

He shook his head. "No, there wasn't anything there. Remember the paint? So, what's the next store you want to go to?"

She groaned. "A second-hand one would probably do."

"I don't have a problem with second-hand anything," he said. "But you don't need to buy second-hand shoes. You might as well invest in something you can wear long term."

Following his urging she went to a popular store several blocks away and picked up a pair of sneakers and a pair of slip-ons on sale. As they walked back out, she said, "Perfect. Now we can go home. And thank you very much for driving me."

"As always you're welcome. You don't need to thank me for every little thing."

She chuckled. "Yes, I do. That's how I was raised."

"Your grandfather again?"

She nodded. "No good deed should go unnoticed. Why don't we go to the police station in town? I'd like to get an update on the police report, and I have to go in and sign statements. It'd be better to get it all done before we head home."

He shrugged and pulled out his phone, punching in the detective's number. It went automatically to voicemail. He shrugged. "Apparently he's busy. We'll put it off for another day." He turned the truck in the direction of the compound.

"Mind if I turn on the radio?"

"Go right ahead."

She played with the remote until she picked up a new station. Over the airwaves they heard, "Breaking news. A prisoner picked up earlier, after breaking and entering a house where he attacked two of the residents, has escaped. Details are slim, but, at this time, the police have posted his photo saying he's armed and dangerous. Do not approach."

"Goddamn it." Dakota pounded the steering wheel. "How the hell did he get loose?"

"Is that the intruder from our house?" She stared at him in shock. "That doesn't make any sense."

"It depends where he escaped from. But he was a pro. He would know the ins and outs of the system and how to free himself again."

"Is he coming back after us?"

"I don't know." Dakota pulled off to the roadside and dialed Levi. "You need to check with the cops. We just heard an alert saying our intruder may have escaped."

Levi's hard voice filled the truck. "We just heard. Yes, it's him. We can't get Mannford on the phone either. Can you run to the Houston police station and see if he's around? If you can't find him, determine when he was last seen."

Dakota pulled the truck back into traffic and made a U-turn. Still on the phone, he asked, "Are we thinking Mannford's involved?"

"Or missing," Levi snapped. "Ice didn't speak with him directly, but she had a message on her machine. She's been trying to get a hold of him since then, but there's been no response at all."

"Give me his home address, and we'll head there first."

Levi rattled off the number and the street.

"I've got it. I know where that is." Dakota turned the truck to the left, then back right. "We'll call you after we arrive."

He put the phone down on the seat beside him. "We need to see if Mannford's around. Levi's afraid he's gone missing."

"With the assailant or dead because of the assailant?"

"We can't go there yet."

With nothing else to do, she sat back and watched, waiting. Inside, her nerves were knotted down tight. This was not what she needed to hear. They picked up one assailant and were looking for the guy who supposedly had shot the mayor. What she didn't need to hear was that both men were on the loose.

DAKOTA PULLED UP in front of a series of brownstone townhomes. The detective's was the end unit. With Bailey at his side, he walked up the steps to the front door and knocked. He followed that up with a ringing of the doorbell. They stood and listened. Nothing. He motioned down the stairs and said, "Let's go around to the back." There he repeated the knocking.

With no answer, he tried to peer through the kitchen window. Bailey did the same on the other side of the door.

"I can't see anything," she exclaimed.

He studied the layout and then his gaze recognized something he knew all too well. "I do," he snapped. He reached into his pocket, pulling out the tool he wanted. He'd picked the lock on the back door in seconds.

"Can we do this?"

He pushed open the door and bolted inside. As he went around the corner of the kitchen he stopped and fell to his knees. Detective Mannford was on his back, blood under his shoulders and neck. Dakota reached down to check for a pulse, his phone automatically in his hand. He dialed emergency and said, "We have a police officer down."

He stared grimly at the man who'd just been at their place only hours earlier. While still on the phone, he said, "Two bullets, one high at the base of his neck." He got off the call and placed a second call to Levi. "Mannford has been shot in his townhouse. He's still alive, but he's in bad shape. Emergency services are on the way, but I don't feel he'll make it." He glanced over at Bailey and said, "I've got Bailey here. I would like to get her home and out of this situation as soon as possible."

"Wait there until the ambulance and the police arrive. Deal with the police, and then we'll look at what's next. Are the premises secured?"

"I haven't had a chance to check," he answered. "I'm holding pressure on one of the wounds. Although it's probably too late to be worried about it."

"Watch your six. You know this is bad news."

Chapter 15

S O MUCH DEATH. Bailey stood over Detective Mannford, staring at the badly injured man.

"Bailey? Bailey?"

She shook her head, coming out of her daze, and turned to stare at Dakota. "What?" she asked.

"Are you okay?" he asked in a sharp tone.

She realized she'd been standing with her hand over her mouth, focused on the poor man. She dropped to her knees at his side and whispered, "Yes, I'm fine. But he's not. There's just been so much death. So much killing."

"Well, he's not dead yet, so we can't write him off."

She nodded. "Is it possible to survive with so much blood loss?"

"I hope so," he said firmly. "I have a bigger concern. I don't know if this place is safe. I don't want you to go anywhere. Just stay here with me."

She stared at him in shock and then quickly spun around, looking into the living room and dining room areas. "Do you think he could be upstairs? His attacker, I mean? Why would he stick around?"

"It's certainly happened before. We've seen break-ins where people killed the owners and then just lived in their house with the dead bodies rotting in the kitchen while the intruders did laundry and cooked a meal. There is no rhyme or reason. In this case, we can't be sure who shot the detective either."

She wrapped her arms around her chest and sat down on the floor against the wall. "How can you live like this?" she whispered. She felt his gaze but didn't dare look at him. "After my husband died, it just seemed like everything was over in my world. There was so much illness, and yet, at the end, death was a release. This isn't like that. This is so much the opposite. It's violence. Anger. Not release and relief."

"We're doing our best to make sure nobody else gets killed."

She nodded. "I understand that. It's just … difficult."

"I know. I'm so sorry you have to see this, to deal with this."

She rolled her head to the side and looked at him. "It's not your fault. You did everything right."

He reached over and gently clasped her hand with his. "You've done nothing wrong either."

"Sure feels like nothing's been right either. For the longest time, I wanted to die with my husband. I knew how much that attitude angered him. He wanted me to live. But just because that's how he felt, he didn't make it easy for me to feel that way."

"Of course your life is about *you* being *you*. It's not about being what other people want you to be. One of the hardest things kids have to do when growing up these days is finding out who they are inside. Not irrationally listening to their peers or being pushed into the wrong things by the masses or otherwise persuaded against their will by the Internet. It's a matter of looking inside and seeing what's right and wrong for *you*."

"Easy to say …"

"But not easy to do," he finished. He nodded. "And it took me a long time to get there myself. Thankfully I have."

"I'm not there yet. I'm not sure how far off I am. Rick told me not to wallow. I wallowed. He told me not to cry. I cried. Grief is a funny thing. It's a hard taskmaster. No matter how much you try to hide from it, it doesn't make any difference. It still comes, grabs you by the throat and makes you deal with it."

"Life is like that too." He grinned. "Besides, you're not alone with dealing with hardship. Most of us here have lost someone. No, not in the same way but it's hard no matter what way."

"I'm sorry," she said sincerely. "I have to keep remembering that I've come through a lot already."

He nodded. "Absolutely. So don't ever knock yourself. Don't feel less than or way worse than anybody else. You've done a damn fine job so far."

She leaned her head against the wall. "Shouldn't the ambulance be here by now?"

The words weren't fully out of her mouth when the sirens could be heard in the distance.

She slowly got to her feet. "I'll open the front door for them."

She walked toward the door and pulled it open just as the police and ambulance arrived. She motioned for them to come straight in. And then she stepped out of the way. She'd forgotten how well-oiled-machine-like emergency calls were. It was amazing to watch how efficient and professional each of them was as they came in to deal with the detective.

A policeman asked her to step to one side. "Can you tell me what happened?"

Bailey motioned toward the kitchen where the detective

lay on the floor beside Dakota. "You should probably ask him. We came looking for the detective after we heard the prisoner had escaped. Last we saw him was when he picked up the prisoner from our home."

The policeman turned to Dakota, caught his eye and motioned for him to join them. Dakota walked over, his hands covered in blood. She couldn't stop staring at them. While the two men talked, she went into the kitchen, found paper towels on the counter, soaked several sheets with water from the tap and took several dry sheets, holding them out for Dakota. He looked down and quickly wiped his hand free of the mess. She took the dirty towels away and put them in the garbage, then washed her hands.

For a long moment, she stood over the sink, hearing the sounds and the noises, but it was the smell of the blood that caught her. Every time she'd had to go in and deal with the bandages and the sores that had developed on Rick's body, she was assaulted with just this sickness, this metallic smell around her husband. It had been hard. As her heart was breaking, his body was decomposing. It had been a massive lesson on life, the fragility of the organic body. Seeing the detective with his blood dripping away had been a brutal reminder.

She heard the orders as he was lifted and carried out. When she figured it was safe, she walked around the kitchen and watched, her breath shaky in her throat.

"Bailey?"

She looked at Dakota as he walked over and wrapped an arm around her, tucking her close. She couldn't help but snuggle in. She wrapped an arm around his back and looped it with her other one. "I hope he'll be okay," she whispered.

He squeezed her gently. "They'll take good care of him.

It's a miracle we got here when we did."

"Now I feel guilty about going shopping," she cried.

"No. Don't. You didn't have a clue. We didn't know until we heard the announcement on the radio."

She nodded. "Still, it doesn't change the fact that, if we'd gotten here earlier, he might have a better chance."

"Don't write him off. Just because he's down does not mean he's out. And, if we hadn't come to town to shop, we wouldn't have come by his place at all. This is not your husband all over again. Just because your husband died does not mean Mannford will."

"A completely different scenario," she muttered. "I know that intellectually, but …"

"Exactly.

"Can we go home now?"

"I have to check in with Levi and see if he wants us to do anything else. But, as far as the police are concerned, we can leave."

He pulled out his phone, called Levi and updated him. Still being held in Dakota's arms, Bailey was close enough to hear the bulk of their conversation. He ended the conversation with, "If there is nothing else, then we'll head home."

"Nothing more you can do," Levi said. "I'd rather have you home safe and sound before anybody else gets hurt."

Dakota pocketed his phone. With his arm still around her, he led her to the truck.

Inside he turned on the heater, instinctively understanding how chilled she was inside. A light rain started. She looked out at the slight drops coming down, hitting the windshield. "It looks like the world knows my mood."

He started up the engine, checked his watch and said, "We don't want to miss dinner, so let's get a move on."

She looked at the time and shook her head. "Brisket should be done. Alfred would've finished the vegetables. We'll get leftovers."

"Good. I love leftovers."

She settled back for the trip home. Forty five minutes later, as they came into the gates, she was surprised to see they were locked. He stopped, waited for a few minutes, then the gates opened automatically, and they drove in. "They can see us?"

"Absolutely. From the control room."

"So nobody can get in unless someone lets them?"

"Not from this direction."

She nodded and settled back. "Yet a man made it inside. Was that because he knew about the tunnel?"

"That means he had some idea from somebody about the blueprints of this place. He also knew where the blind spot was. He took the camera out there. All in all, like I said, he was a pro. The chances of us meeting up with too many pros like him are pretty rare."

"Maybe he is angry you captured him. What are the chances he's looking for payback?"

"I doubt payback is the issue. Although that doesn't mean he won't try again," Dakota admitted.

"Are we safe here?"

"I won't lie. It's pretty damn hard to stay safe when you've got a professional killer after you. But you're safer here than you would possibly be elsewhere."

She sighed. "I could have gone to a hotel. He wouldn't have known where I was."

"What makes you think he wouldn't follow you? What makes you think he isn't still following us now?"

She spun to look in the direction they'd come, almost

crying out at the immediate wrenching of her back. "Is he?"

"No. Nobody followed us out of town."

"But you were watching for that, weren't you?"

He nodded. "Absolutely."

They walked inside to find everybody sitting down and eating. She took her place, smiled at Alfred and said, "I'm so sorry for not getting back in time to help with the vegetables."

"Much better you helped Mannford get to the hospital."

She ate, even though she wasn't hungry. She understood the value of food, but it was hard when Mannford was in the hospital, fighting for his life. "I hate waiting for updates. I hate waiting for doctors to contact you with test results. I hate waiting in the hospital for somebody to talk to you." Her sudden words out of context startled the group.

Dakota reached across and gently stroked her shoulder. "We'll get an update on him tonight."

Slightly embarrassed, she lowered her face and kept eating.

Levi spoke up. "Dakota, you want to tell us what you saw?"

"AFTER WE HEARD the news on the radio, I called you, diverted toward Mannford's place. It's actually a condo. The front door was locked, so we went around to the back. The kitchen door was locked. We both looked in the windows on either side of the door. I could see his foot, lying on the floor. I picked the lock, went in and found him on the floor with two bullet holes, one in the neck, one in the chest. I placed my fingers on the bullet hole in his chest. The severe bleeding slowed, then his pulse slowed and grew weak, and blood came from the neck wound."

"Not arterial?" Ice asked.

Dakota shook his head. "But I don't know how long he was there. I don't know how severe the blood loss was."

She nodded. "If they can stem the flow and get him stabilized, infusions will help him to recover. All depends on how extensive the damage was."

"It didn't look like either hit a vital organ," Bailey said quietly. "Also I saw no damage to the living room. No furniture was tossed. No drawers in the kitchen had been left opened, and there was no sign of a disturbance. It's as if someone just walked in and shot him."

"Except," Ice said, "the door was locked."

Bailey stopped and stared at her. "Yes," she said slowly, "it was."

"Someone had keys to the place or took his and locked the doors behind him."

Dakota, his voice hard, said, "Or one other alternative— he was still inside."

Bailey swallowed hard. "I did tell the officer we didn't have a chance to do a search of the house. I think one of the EMTs said he'd been shot at least an hour before we arrived."

"The blood was already starting to congeal," Dakota added quietly.

Ice nodded. "Depending on a lot of different factors, that could've happened at various times."

Bailey turned toward Dakota. "That's why you didn't want me to leave your side? In case the shooter was still in the house?"

He nodded. "If he remained in the detective's house, the shooter had to know someone would show up sometime."

There was silence around the table, everyone taking in what Dakota said.

"He could have gotten out any number of ways, including windows on the second floor. We've done something similar many times," Levi said quietly. "Let's not get hung up on how he may have been inside still. I highly doubt he was still there otherwise he'd have taken you both out, needing to make sure he left no witnesses behind. Particularly after having shot a detective."

After a few minutes Dakota finished off his plate, pushed it to one side and said, "What about us going after this guy?"

"Is it one guy or two guys?" Ice countered.

"Two guys," Bailey said. "The one who shot the man in the alley, and the man you captured here." She turned to look at Levi. "Do we know if the mayor survived?"

"He'll be fine. He's expected to be released from the hospital today."

Just then a figure appeared in the doorway. Dakota looked up and grinned. "Merk, you've got a hell of a hard head."

Merk took several steps slowly toward the table and sat down. "Maybe not hard enough." He growled. "Who the hell hit me?"

"An intruder. He came through the tunnel. You opened the door and went out, but he was already there. He didn't know you were coming out, but he caught you right at the edge."

"Asshole. My head still hurts."

Katina came in behind him and sat down, her hand gripping Merk's. "He was too stubborn. He wouldn't stay in bed."

"You wouldn't stay with me," he said. "No way in hell

I'm staying down there alone."

She shook her head. "Like I said, stubborn."

Dakota watched the two of them, seeing how she hovered over him, but she let him do his own thing. Lots to be said for that attitude.

Merk straightened up and said, "Please tell me that you caught him."

Levi nodded. "We caught him. Had him picked up by Detective Mannford. He was transferred to the local jail. And he escaped. On top of that, Mannford has been shot twice in his own home."

Merk's jaw dropped. "I've been knocked over the head, and the world goes to shit."

"Also the mayor was shot," Bailey added. "Just to add to the confusion."

Merk looked down the table at her. "Say what?"

Ice stepped in. "The mayor was shot high in the shoulder. The wound was superficial, and he was released from the hospital."

"Lucky bastard," Merk said. He stared over at the coffeepot and then at Katina.

Without a word, she stood up, poured him a cup, returned to the table and gave it to him, then went back and poured one for herself. "Thank you." He leaned over and kissed her on the cheek. "What will we do about this shit? I'm tired of getting hit. As far as I'm concerned, instead of waiting, we need to attack," Merk said.

That started the discussion all over again. "We know the attacker is on the FBI wanted list. His known associates are the drug cartel world. Who hired him here will make for an interesting connection," Levi said.

"By now he's gone underground," Merk said. "Can we

check into the city traffic cams, see where he might have gone?" he asked Ice.

"Stone's already checking on that."

"Wouldn't it be easier for him to go to somebody's empty house and stay there?" Bailey asked.

Dakota shook his head. "I doubt he'll do something like that. A pro like this will have a couple aliases registered and go to a hotel."

Merk asked. "Are we on high alert in case of a second attempt?"

"Absolutely," Levi said.

"Speaking of which, it's time to relieve Stone in the control room." Ice stood and grabbed a cup of coffee and walked from the room.

Dakota watched her go. As soon as she left, silence settled. Several of the women got up and walked out.

Bailey patted Dakota's hand and said, "I'll go help Alfred in the kitchen."

She got up, leaving Dakota alone with the other men. Perfect. Now they could make plans.

Chapter 16

"I 'M ALMOST FINISHED here in the kitchen," Alfred said. "You don't need to help me."

She smiled. "I think the men wanted to talk."

He nodded. "Making more plans."

"Can't say I'd be much help with that." She walked over to the commercial dishwasher. "However, I do know what to do with this."

He chuckled. "Then have at it."

They worked in companionable silence for a few moments, and then she said, "Do you think he'll likely try again?"

"Yes, I do."

"Oh." She said in a small voice. "Maybe it's better for me to leave."

"It won't change anything. Besides Dakota won't let you."

She nodded. "I guess that makes sense." She kept working away, looking for an answer to this mess.

"You don't need to feel guilty. This is what these men do. They are in there making plans. Pretty soon someone will fill us in."

She gave him a sideways look. "The men will come get you. I'm nothing."

He gave a chuckle. "You're a big part of this."

Sure enough, Dakota came to the kitchen and said, "Alfred, Bailey, we need you in here for a moment."

The two walked into the dining room.

Levi had a roster on the table and was going over it with the others. "Run four-hour shifts, security outside."

"Why outside?"

"Because, despite our best efforts, we can't get that camera in the blind spot back working today. So, somebody will be on the hill always. Four-hour shifts."

Bailey popped up and said, "I can do that."

Dakota snorted. "Why? So he can pick you off on the hill right off the bat?"

"Sure." She glared at him. "It's better than him picking you guys off."

"Nobody will be picking anybody off," Levi said. "But these men here are trained for this, and you're not, Bailey." His tone of voice was gentle, kind.

She appreciated the consideration. At the same time she wanted to contribute. "Can I help in any way?"

He shook his head. "No, I don't want you wandering around the building from this moment on. Seven o'clock on, you need to stay in your room."

She nodded. "I can do that."

"If there's any disturbance at all, you're to pair up and stay with somebody. We do not want anybody unaccounted for. Twelve of us are on this compound at this moment. Make sure we know where all twelve are every moment of the day."

"Should we pair up now?" Bailey asked. "That way we always have an eye on somebody else."

"Technically that would work," Levi admitted. "Most of

them will be paired up anyway, since I'm pulling men to run the four-hour shifts."

"And the women have roles to play when we need them too. Most prefer to stay locked in their rooms, waiting for the men to come back," Ice stated calmly. "But they are on call if we need them."

Ice was running a shift in the control room. But other than that, Bailey was alone. Alfred was alone. Dakota was alone, but she wasn't sure anybody else here was. She still didn't have a handle on who lived here permanently as half the crew was gone on vacation or on a mission.

They discussed a few other issues; then Levi set up the schedule. Dakota would be outside on sentry duty, and Ice was in the control room on security detail. Stone was inside security; then he would relieve Dakota as sentry.

All that information running through her head made her more than a little nervous. Only one thing she could do—stay out of the way. She was more than willing to do that. She had her tablet, so she would find something to do.

Back in her room she sat down, wishing she'd had a chance to say good-bye to Dakota. To tell him to be careful. But he'd disappeared with Levi to talk about weapons. She understood now a full armory existed in the compound. Instead of making her nervous, it reassured her. The men were all trained to use any of those weapons.

She'd never seen anything like this. Or been surrounded by warriors like she was. She couldn't imagine what this place was like when it was full up. She kept hearing they had several men out on jobs. And a couple women were away on business, and one was visiting family. All in all, it would be quite a family gathering when they came back. Of course

Bailey wouldn't be here that long.

She had a lot of decisions to make about her own future. She was still okay with her job, as far she knew. She did feel a sense of freedom not having a lot of belongings anymore, but the mess at her apartment still had to be cleaned up.

Luckily she had saved the items from her husband.

Thinking of that, she walked over to the box she'd brought back. She opened the lid with the photos and the memories. She smiled when she saw their wedding photo. He looked so healthy and happy. Little did they know he was already very sick inside. He had no pain. Never showed any discomfort.

By the time she got to the bottom of the box she was sniffling, but it was no longer with the same heartache, the same ripping agony going through her soul. And neither was she bawling. That was progress.

There was a knock on her door.

"Come in."

Dakota stepped inside, smiled at her, saw the box in her hand, and his smile fell away.

She put the box off to the side. "You are heading out?"

He nodded. "I am. I'll be out four hours. Will I see you when I get back?"

"No, I'll be asleep by then."

He walked over to her. "Are you okay? You were upset earlier."

She shifted gently for her back's sake. "Actually I'm feeling okay about it all. I'm still sorry for the detective though. Even though the intruder managed to get in last night, I'm feeling safe. Except that I'm not sure about you."

He raised an eyebrow. "What about me?"

"You'll be walking to the top of the hill, looking to see if anybody is coming at us, yet you'll possibly end up being a victim too."

He shook his head. "I won't be a victim. We are all trained, so don't worry. This is what I do. This is what we all do."

She gave him a quick glance. "I know all that, but shit happens."

He chuckled. "Shit does happen, and it happens often, but we know that. We expect that."

She slowly stood up. "Any chance of a hug before you go?"

He opened his arms. "Actually that's what I came for."

She gave him a delighted smile. "Glad to hear it." She walked into his arms, and for a long moment they just stood in peaceful silence.

He stepped back. "Stay in here, and stay safe." He chucked her on the chin.

She smiled, repeated the gesture under his chin and said, "Stay safe outside."

He leaned over and kissed her on her forehead and walked out.

She watched as the door closed. And realized just how very wrong that kiss from him was. It hadn't been a kiss of a lover. It hadn't even necessarily been a kiss of a friend. Instead it was almost fatherly. As if he wanted to show he cared but didn't feel he could do more than a chaste kiss to her head. That was so wrong.

She sat back down and thought about the changes she'd been through, the turmoil she'd been through, and how far she'd come.

Then she realized she hadn't really let him know she was over her husband's death. So far he'd been extremely circumspect in looking after her. Sure, she had no idea if the interest was there on both sides. But he'd never in any way shown himself to be seriously interested in her, as if he was just waiting for her to encourage him. He was interested but not ready to do anything about it.

Confused, not sure what she was saying to herself, she realized the real issue was the fact she was pretty sure he thought she wasn't ready for another relationship. That she was still grieving for her husband.

And he was wrong. But he wouldn't know that. She glanced down at the box on the bed and smiled. If one good thing had come from this madness, this drama had helped her look at the last few years and all she'd gone through to understand she was ready to move on.

SOME NIGHTS YOU can see forever, where the moonlight splashed across the ground, showing you every rock, every hill, every dip in the ground. With such clarity you could hike for miles. Tonight was not one of those nights. It was hard going in the darkness. Dakota wasn't quite as familiar with the terrain as the others were. But he knew perfectly well where he should be and shouldn't be as he hunkered down around the brush near the entrance to the tunnel, his eyes adjusting to the darkness.

Running lights in the tunnel were both good and bad. They were great for seeing where you were going, but they also posed a problem because, while your eyes adjusted to the half-light, you were momentarily blind as you stepped out of the tunnel into a night like tonight.

He was in the clear. No vehicle was below, although he didn't know what was going on with the camera still.

He tapped his comm twice to give the signal, then settled down to wait. He was on the top of the peak, the tunnel just below him, bushes to the side, and he had a view of the road as it wandered toward town.

As he sat, he let his mind drift to thoughts of Bailey, her husband, Detective Mannford and the mayor. Instead of tumbling and jumbling in his mind, he let the thoughts pass through. He looked at each one quietly and let them slip on by. His brain operated better that way.

Thankfully it was dry outside. With the hard rain that had been flashing back and forth the last couple days, he was happy to see the ground was dusty again. It was easier to hear footsteps in the wild when conditions were dry. With his months of SEAL training, he had learned to be as quiet and stealthy as any of the animals that lived and hunted beside them.

In the far distance, he could see vehicle lights as they headed toward the little nearby town. Both going in opposite directions. Dakota was just high enough to see the beams of light as they traveled on the main roads. But nothing came down this way. It didn't mean somebody wasn't coming on foot though.

He let his gaze drift over the hillsides, stopping when he noticed movement. He caught the hint of more activity, though he wasn't sure what he had found. Other animals would be out hunting. But he knew in his gut the one they were looking for would show tonight.

There was still the mayor issue too. Dakota wished there

was a follow-up on the henchman. He was looking a little too much like a patsy in the shooting of the mayor too. Not that Dakota hated politicians, but he hated politics in general and found most politicians to be liars. He knew honest ones were out there in the world, but he'd yet not been honored to meet one. Still, he had to keep an open mind.

He just couldn't stop thinking that maybe the mayor had shot himself. It was a hard shot to make. There would be GSR on his hand, and the wound would look very different if the gun barrel had been pressed against the skin.

It should be easy enough for the police to look into. And the mayor wasn't stupid. Maybe he'd hired somebody to take care of shooting him in the shoulder. With two men still on the run, it could be either one of them that showed up tonight again. Dakota doubted there'd be a third person involved. Two gunmen not working together were already two too many.

Dakota loved being outdoors, being one with the land. He was comfortable with his job, comfortable with the skills he used naturally. Yet there was always more he'd like to learn. What he did, he did well.

He was considering shifting his position when something moved into the area of his sight. He watched as a coyote picked his way across the brush. Dakota was still adjusting to the native wildlife of Texas versus California, but coyotes were everywhere here.

Turning his head ever-so-slightly he checked the area to his left. He didn't use binoculars but had brought up his rifle scope. The glint of the moonlight was not much but still enough to give away his position. A pro would also see any movement he made. Still, he needed to check the position behind him.

He slowly sank back to the ground behind the brush and then twisted to look behind him. All was clear. But it didn't feel clear. His instincts still plowed into his stomach, nudging, poking and prodding him.

He knew Bailey would be tucked up in bed. And he had to admit he'd love to be there with her. At least to just hold her and let her know she was safe. He had to move cautiously. She was a long way from being ready for a relationship. He wasn't sure he was the patient type. But he would find out. There was just something about her. Something about her smile. He also didn't know if she was *interested* in him. She was leaning on him, accepting the help he could provide. Although she'd been resistant at the beginning, she certainly felt comfortable accepting everyone's help now.

She had also stepped up and had been a trooper helping Alfred. That she loved to cook and was obviously a gifted chef was just another plus on her side. He knew she'd fit in. In fact, she'd fit in beautifully. He wondered if Levi would consider hiring her as help for Alfred. But then Dakota didn't know if that was what she wanted. It was part of her history. Maybe she had walked away from it and was happy to stay away. Helping somebody out in a pinch was a whole different story than taking it on as a career again.

But it would keep her close. It would keep her where he could slowly work on developing a relationship with her. He tossed it around in his mind, wondering if Levi would hire Bailey to help Alfred.

Dakota had to admit his reasons were selfish, and Levi would know it. No matter what arguments Dakota came up with, Levi and Ice would know. Hell, everyone would know.

An hour into his four-hour session, he tapped his comm twice to let them know he was still here and still fine. With his eyes ever watching, another hour passed by quietly. By the time he came to the end of his four-hour shift, he wondered if his instincts had been off.

Until a bush not too far off moved. He froze, then pivoted behind the bushes to peer down the hillside where he'd heard the sound. Nothing moved. Then a long figure detached itself and climbed again. Dakota tapped his comm three times and three times again to let his team know company was coming.

He let his focus settle on the intruder. He was too far away to determine if it was the same person as last time. But the guy moved silently. Low to the ground. Swiftly, surely crossing the distance to the compound. He hadn't driven so he'd come cross-country. But had he come alone? Without losing track of his quarry, Dakota searched the hills to the side.

From a tap in his earpiece, he understood Rhodes had taken a position on the far side. Their quarry would be sandwiched between them. Only Dakota was at the entrance point where the intruder appeared to be heading. Rhodes would come up behind him, and they'd pinch him in place. At least that was the plan. Dakota watched, never taking his gaze from the man as he moved closer, silent and as deadly as any predator of the night.

Stone and Ice would've picked him up on camera by now. Dakota waited. They should have another man inside the tunnel, but they were running short on staff. He shifted closer then hunkered down. As it was, it would be awkward to pull himself out of hiding before the intruder pulled the tunnel door open. A warm glow immediately lit up his profile. Good he didn't know about the kill switch for the running lights.

The intruder revealed the small handgun he kept almost hidden within the palm of his hand.

Just as the intruder stepped inside the tunnel, rifles were cocked.

Levi's hard voice called, "I don't think so."

Instantly Dakota was behind the man, his own handgun pressed against the man's lower spine. He removed the handgun from the intruder and pocketed it. Then he slipped off the assault rifle from the man's shoulder and shifted it over his own. To Levi, Dakota said, "I've got a gun on him, taken his weapons."

"All clear," Ice said.

By the time Levi had searched the intruder and had handcuffs on his wrists, Rhodes had joined them. With one last glance into the darkness around them, they moved the intruder inside the house and downstairs to the jail.

Dakota wanted to believe this was now over. But he had a nagging doubt that the asshole had come alone. Usually pros worked alone. Not only did they not have to share the paycheck but nobody could double-cross them. But nothing about this was straightforward so far.

With the man unarmed, and all his weapons broken down into pieces, it would take at least a few minutes to put them back together, in case he somehow got free and grabbed one of them. Dakota turned his attention to the intruder. Levi pulled off the full-face mask. And they all froze. It was not the previous intruder. It was yet another stranger.

"Oh, shit." Levi jogged to the side wall for the intercom. Dakota snapped up his weapons and said, "I'm on it." He raced back upstairs and checked the main floor. Into his comm he said, "Ice, did anybody else come through of the tunnel?"

"No, not that we've seen. But we should add sensors in there at first chance. What's the matter?"

"It's not the previous intruder. It's a stranger."

He could hear her shocked silence. "We'll do a full sweep upstairs and move down each floor, but we haven't seen any other intruder enter."

"No guarantee there is a second one, but this doesn't feel right. I'll head back to the outside tunnel entrance and make sure everything is secured. Levi and Rhodes have this guy."

"After this we are putting in a proper jail," Ice snapped. "One where nobody can get the hell out."

As he raced along the tunnel, Dakota understood how she felt. It was one thing to catch these guys, but to lose them again and have to recatch them was a pain in the ass. He slipped out into the night once again. It took a good ten minutes to search the hills, but the night felt empty. He knew he could be wrong, but he was itching to go back inside and check the house.

Even though Ice had been looking for an intruder, she may have taken her gaze off the tunnel entrance for just a moment. Even a long blink was all it took sometimes. What they needed was an extra lock so, even if somebody came in the tunnel, they couldn't get into the house. Like a secondary defense.

He tapped his comm. "I'm coming back in, Ice."

Just as he was about to open the tunnel door to the main

floor of the house, his comm went off three times and another three times. Under his breath he whispered, "Shit."

Chapter 17

BAILEY NAPPED UNTIL she rolled over the wrong way, and something in her back sent sharp pains rippling through her ribs. Instantly she awoke, gasping for the waves of torture to slow down. There was only so much pain she could take. Apparently she'd hit her limit. She'd forgotten to take the painkillers before going to bed.

Crap. Awake now, she slowly sat up and made her way to the bathroom. When she was done, she sat back down on the bed, took two painkillers, washing them down with a drink of water. Her stomach felt oddly queasy too. She frowned, wondering if it was okay to go to the kitchen to get a glass of warm milk. She knew Alfred wouldn't mind, but she was supposed to stay in her room. Still she'd be there and back in ten minutes. She could bring the cup to her room.

With everybody on watch, she figured it was safe. She put her feet inside her slippers, tossed on her robe, wincing at the pain, knowing she would need Ice to see if any stitches had been ripped out. Although how she could've possibly done that, she didn't know.

Out in the hall she quietly made her way to the elevator.

She was still tying the sash around her bathrobe when the doors opened on her floor. She inspected it before stepping inside and headed downstairs.

This place was more like a hotel than a home. But it had

a very homey feel. Ice and Levi had done a wonderful job making it something others felt welcome in.

In the kitchen, she went to the refrigerator for the milk and poured some in a saucepan, quickly heating it up on the stove. It didn't take long before she poured it into her mug. She added a cinnamon stick and returned to the hallway.

She'd overfilled her mug slightly, making it hard to walk without spilling. At the elevator doors, she pressed the button and waited. She blew on the top of the milk in her cup, wishing it would cool. The cup itself was heating up. Why hadn't she thought to bring a tray?

The door opened, and she stepped gently inside, not wishing to spill milk or someone might slip and fall. As she went to close the door, somebody joined her. She glanced up with a smile, only to have her smile fall away. "What are you doing here?"

"Bailey? Bailey Hoskins?" the mayor asked. He gave her a smarmy politician smile filled with arrogance that said he could do whatever the hell he wanted to do to her. She pressed the button to keep the door open.

When she went to step back out again, he said, "Oh, I don't think so." He flipped the switch that held the elevator indefinitely. A pause button. With no harsh buzzing noises.

Her heart sinking, she knew this wasn't good, and she had no idea where anybody else was. "How did you get in?"

"When they captured my buddy, they forgot to close the hatch behind them." He chuckled. "All the focus was on my bogey and not on me."

"I'm sure they are still looking for you." She glared at him. "Everyone is looking for you after you shot the detective."

"Absolutely. But I didn't shoot the detective. That was

Jim, one of my men. And it doesn't matter because I don't give a shit about him. He served his purpose."

"What? To get rid of your enemies? Did you kill Jim too? He's gone missing, so I bet you have, haven't you? I know politics is cutthroat, but that's ridiculous. Especially as he killed your other man in the alleyway, Troy Burgess? Why? Why kill anyone?"

"Troy was all for a deal we had going, but then he got cold feet. I couldn't have that," the mayor said in a hard voice. "So he had to be dealt with before he went to the cops. The best way to keep people on your side is to embroil them in the conflicts so they can't run to the police. Jim has been taking care of ugly business for a long time. We expect to get paid for the government contracts we hand out. All of us expect something. And the more the better." He grinned. "Then there are the deals to look the other way while companies did illegal things. We all knew there was a price tag. But then a building collapsed and killed a couple children. It probably wouldn't have happened if we'd made sure the inspection was done. But Jim had actually been the one to push it through. He couldn't stomach the results. So one day Jim decided he wanted out."

"And you shot yourself as a diversion." She glared at him. "No one was fooled."

"Doesn't matter as I didn't do it. My new hired man was very helpful that way."

She snorted. "Does he know he was the diversion?"

The mayor shrugged his shoulders. He had massive shoulders, and she realized he had more of a linebacker's build. "How did you get so close to the property without anyone seeing you?"

He smiled. "You ask so many questions."

She shook her head. "I know they didn't see any vehicle on the road, or they would've seen you."

"I've been in Texas a long time, little girl. There are a whole lot more ways of getting things done than you might think."

She frowned at him. "And what are you doing here?"

"Well, you and I will have a talk."

She slipped out, but he grabbed her free arm. "No games. Absolutely no games."

"I'm not going into that elevator with you."

"Yes, you are." And he pulled her closer.

She used the only weapon she had. Boiled milk. She threw it directly at his face. His screams of rage and pain were music to her ears.

She raced down the stairs to the prisoner holding cell. Someone would be standing guard. She didn't know where else to run. She could have gone to the control room, but she didn't want to lead the mayor upstairs where some of the others would be sleeping.

She heard the mayor running behind her and picked up the pace. Her back was injured, not her legs, but every jump she made down the stairs sent jarring pain up her back. She bolted through the door, shouting. Merk stepped out and grabbed her. "What's the matter?"

"He's chasing me," she babbled. "He just grabbed me at the elevator. I threw hot milk in his face and ran."

She was shaking so badly she could hardly stand. Merk tucked her up behind him and pushed them both behind the door.

She didn't have a weapon now. She'd used the only one available to her, but she really wanted something else. She glanced over at the prisoner, staring at them with a big smirk on his face.

She glared at him. "I wouldn't be smiling. You were the diversion. He didn't give a shit if you got caught or not."

The smile fell away. He glared at her. "Like hell. He's here to rescue me."

"Dream on. He's here to do the job you couldn't do."

Merk reached around and grabbed her hand and gave her a warning to be quiet. Across the way she could see the medical clinic. She slipped past the prisoner and into the clinic. Crouching low behind a stretcher, she neared where they kept the medical instruments. What a well-stocked facility. Lots of needles. She had no idea if she could fill one with drugs and then plunge it into the mayor's arm. But, even with a scalpel in her hand, knowing it was deadly sharp, she felt better.

Suddenly there was gunfire. She raced to the doorway and sank down behind the little cabinet. She hoped Merk was okay. He already had a head injury. The last thing he needed was to get hurt again.

The gunfire filled her head. She could hear other people racing toward them. But she just wasn't sure who. She peered around the door. The first thing she saw was the prisoner. Then she gasped at the sudden movement to her right as pain surged through her back. There was more gunfire. She crouched back down again, hearing the prisoner taunting Merk.

"You might as well give up. You can't kill the mayor," he said. "You have morals, ethics. He doesn't. He'll kill every person in this house and not give a damn."

"I can kill any asshole intruding into my place that I want," Merk said. "I don't have to take shit from you at all."

"You should listen to my man." The mayor chuckled.

"Or not. Kill him. Then when he's dead, nobody would know who did what."

The prisoner gasped. "Hey, that's not—"

A single shot fired. Silence followed. Bailey peered around the corner to see blood running down the side of the prisoner's head as he now slumped forward in his chair.

She shuddered and closed her eyes. The mayor had killed yet another of his men.

Bailey shook her head. If he would come just a little bit closer, she'd kill him herself.

He stepped in front of the clinic's doorway. "Where is she? I know she came down here."

"I have no idea," Merk said.

She couldn't see Merk anywhere, so she figured he was hiding. The mayor was behind the open door of the medical clinic with his back to her. She glanced down at the scalpel in her hand. She had no idea if it was enough to stab him with. He was a big man. He wouldn't go down with one blow. Unless she went for his neck.

He sent up another shot. And she heard Merk swear. That just made her angry.

Another voice was added to the fray. "Now you're surrounded."

She grinned. That was Dakota.

"Oh, I don't think so. You see? Your little honey is in here with me. So you won't get a chance at her at all."

"Bailey, run," Dakota called.

She didn't know what to do. Answer him or stay quiet?

"Answer me if you're there."

And she realized he wanted to scare the mayor. Make him believe she wasn't in here. All he needed was that split second for the mayor to let his guard down.

The mayor chuckled. "See? She doesn't listen either."

Another shot was fired. It hit the sign on the door beside the mayor. He swore and ducked into the medical clinic, looking around for her.

She was crouched behind the one tiny cabinet. It wouldn't take him long to find her. But the longer he was stuck inside, the more time Merk and Dakota had to get closer.

She held her breath and kept her position low.

"Where are you, little bitch?"

Well, she hadn't answered Dakota, and she certainly would in no way answer him.

The mayor then caught sight of her. A horrible grin spread across his face. He lined up for the shot. She shoved the cabinet his way and bolted to the side under the surgical table. His shot went wild. She came up behind him as he tried to shoot again and slashed at her target.

He screamed at her. Dakota yelled at her. Shots were fired. The door opened behind her, but she couldn't stop slashing. The next thing she knew, strong arms were around her, lifting her and pulling her, holding her up where she couldn't hurt anybody. She heard grunting and moaning and screaming. "Easy, honey. Take it easy, Bailey."

She froze. "Is it over?" she cried. Still twisting, only now registering her back was on fire.

Dakota slowly lowered her to the ground. She turned to see the mayor standing but needing Merk's help to stay on his feet. She'd stabbed his chest, opening his shirt, and he was bleeding from at least a dozen places. One of them was deep in his forearm.

The room filled with people. Ice walked over, took one look at the mayor, assessed the damage and went to Bailey.

She gently held out her hand. "Bailey, I need the scalpel."

Bailey raised her terrified gaze to Ice. "Did I kill him?"

Ice shook her head. "No. We have him now. He can't hurt you again." She moved her hand closer. "I need the scalpel now please."

Slowly, her arm trembling, Bailey reached out and dropped the scalpel in Ice's hand. And that's when she realized she was completely covered in blood—head to toe. She stared down at herself and asked, "Am I hurt?"

Ice chuckled. "I don't know. Are you?"

She looked at Dakota, then looked back at Ice. "I think I'm okay, but my back … On the other hand, the mayor …"

He was sitting now, weak from lack of blood. Ice moved over and put pressure on some of the worst wounds. Levi was on his phone, calls being made, more swearing as others arrived. But it was just too much noise and confusion and chaos.

Before she realized it, Bailey was sitting on a chair. Dakota stood beside her, holding her in place so she didn't collapse. She glanced down at her hands and her bathrobe. "I'm covered in blood."

"It doesn't matter," he said. "I'm just damn glad it's all his."

She shook her head. "All I wanted was a cup of milk."

He glanced at her and over at the mayor. "Is that what's all over his face?"

She took a good look at the mayor's face. It was red, sore-looking, and puffy.

"He got into the elevator with me. When I tried to get out, he came after me. The only thing I had was the cup of hot milk, so I threw it right in his face."

"Good. I hope it was damn hot."

She gave him a glimmer of a smile. "It was." She smirked. "I make a mean warm milk."

He chuckled. His chuckles became louder and louder until he laughed uproariously. He snagged her in his arms, holding her close. "You are a mean machine, one way or another."

She looked up at him and smiled, wrapping her arms around him. "I can't say I've ever been put to the test before."

"You have now, and you passed with flying colors."

She grinned. "Well, I couldn't let him attack you."

He chuckled again. "You're my hero."

She snorted. "You really think I don't know about that? I heard from one of the ladies about the hero joke."

Dakota laughed again. "That's only a joke."

"I don't think so," she said. "If we're to have a relationship, somebody has to be the hero."

"Like hell," he said. "Besides, you're not ready for a relationship. You still miss your husband." With that he shooed her over to where the other ladies stood. "You want to help her get changed and tucked into bed again? We have to talk with these guys and to the cops when they get here."

Sienna nodded, wrapped an arm around Bailey and said, "Come on, mighty warrior. Let's get you to bed."

DAKOTA'S MIND WENT to what Bailey had said. Was she really ready for a relationship? He wasn't exactly sure what her comment meant. He'd seen her sitting on the bed with the box of keepsakes, crying for her dead husband. Dakota didn't want a partial relationship; he wanted a whole one. And, for that, he would have to wait. He didn't have a problem with that. He just preferred to know how long.

The days went by with him at her side, ready but hesitant to make a move.

In the meantime, Detective Mannford improved. Jim had been found dead in his apartment. The ballistics matched the gun the mayor had brought into the compound. The mayor didn't have great working relationships.

Bailey had taken the news in a steady manner. Dakota had been expecting her to pack and leave even as he was looking for excuses to keep her here. He'd even asked Ice if they were looking to hire some help for Alfred.

Instead of giving him an answer, she'd looked at him with amusement and walked out.

Was that a yes or a no?

Chapter 18

BAILEY WATCHED HER relationship with Dakota move from friends to the special friends' area through the next couple days, but then it plateaued.

The compound was slowly returning to normal. Except for her. Sure enough, she'd done something to her back. Ice had been busy helping Bailey heal. Ice and Dakota had vetoed Bailey's suggestion to move out as she didn't have an apartment to go to.

"The least you can do is stay here for another few days so we can make sure you're all better. Once the stitches are out and the wound is closed over, then we'll talk," Ice scolded her.

"If you don't mind me being in the way."

"No, and you aren't in the way. You've been helping Alfred every day."

"I know, and I have really enjoyed it. But I have to go back to work."

Ice nodded. "It's not very far to drive there and come home here, is it?"

"No, but it feels odd. It's not my home."

Ice settled back and patted Bailey's leg. "Okay, you can sit up again."

Bailey sat up slowly. She was in the medical clinic with Ice to change the dressing yet again. She lowered her shirt.

Ice said, "How happy are you with your job?"

Bailey looked at Ice in surprise. "It's okay. It's not my favorite, but it's a job that pays the rent."

"Are you happy working with Alfred?"

Bailey's face lit up. "I love working with Alfred." And her smile fell away just as quickly. "But being here as a guest versus being here as an employee and not part of the company ... Now that wouldn't be the same thing."

Ice tilted her head. "I don't understand how it could be different."

"Because I wouldn't be eating with you at the table ... I don't know. It would just be different."

"You certainly would eat with us at the table, just like Alfred does. You would be one of us in all ways. You would have to train for when we had emergencies. You would be given specific jobs to do when we had security breaches, like everybody else. Everyone has a station they are responsible for. When you're here, it doesn't matter whether the work is in the kitchen, flying helicopters or working on weapons training. You would still be part of the company."

Bailey stared at her in surprise. "Really?"

Ice nodded. "However, I don't want to make you uncomfortable in terms of you and Dakota."

Bailey winced. "Dakota thinks I'm not ready for a relationship. He thinks I'm still mourning my husband."

"Are you?"

Bailey looked at Ice. "That's one thing about you. You're very direct."

"It makes things simpler," Ice said comfortably. "Now no dodging the question. Are you?"

Bailey shook her head. "No, I don't think so. I really want to move forward in a relationship with Dakota, but he's friend-zoned me." She ended that statement with a laugh. "Maybe he doesn't care."

Ice nodded. "Maybe you just need to find out for sure."

"Maybe. That's not necessarily who I am."

Ice picked up the empty packaging and turned to clean up. "That's who you were. Who you are now that you've started this whole new life is someone very different. It's up to you to decide what part of your personality that you'll keep." Ice walked to the exit and smiled at her. "Think about it."

"Think about what? Working with Alfred or Dakota?"

"Both."

The next day was Monday. And her first day back at work. Dakota had offered to drive her as her car was still in the underground parking of her apartment building.

It was early when they arrived at her car. She got out. He checked that everything was okay, and then they said a quick good-bye. She got into her car and drove to work.

It felt better to have her own wheels. It gave her some independence again. She walked most of the time when she lived in the apartment, but now that she was so far out of town, it was nice to drive. Although it felt odd resting her back on the seat. It would be another four or five days likely before her stitches could come out. Until then the strings and bandages would irritate. But as the situation could be much worse, she didn't feel she could complain.

She walked into work and headed for her office. That was one of the things about this job; it was very isolated. She had her own office and rarely did people stop by to see her. She got emails, invoices, requisitions and receipts and spent a lot of her day on the phone. She sat down and reoriented herself to the change in her world again.

Of course, after a week away, she had an awful lot to catch up on. She slowly moved through the backlog. By noon she still hadn't seen anybody else.

She picked up the phone and called HR to let them know she was in the office. They noted it on her chart, but no one said anything else. Several hundred people were employed by the company, making her just a number. It made her realize she was nobody here. Someone who filled a job description, did certain duties and carried on. She wondered if anybody had noticed she hadn't been here for a week.

By the time the end of the day rolled around, she was tired and stressed. There was a lot of work to be done here. Not only had nobody stepped in to do any of the work but customers were angry because Bailey hadn't answered their emails. The company hadn't so much as set up a Vacation Response on her email, saying she would be gone for a week, nor had anybody stopped by to post something on her door to let her coworkers know of her temporary absence.

She'd had to deal with several irate people when they realized she hadn't gotten back to them or hadn't ordered what they had assumed she'd ordered just because they'd sent an email.

When she walked out at the end of the day, she was tired, frustrated and wondering why she'd chosen a job that isolated her so much. It was amazing how angry people could be in an email. And she'd had several of those today.

She got into her car and slowly made her way to the compound. The drive was roughly fifty minutes. It would get slightly faster when she understood the routes and was comfortable with the road. But when she considered how tired she was, it added to her already long day.

She parked outside and walked in. When she checked her watch, it was 4:45. That meant Alfred had been working in the kitchen alone all day. She hurried in to see where he was. She found him, industriously mashing potatoes. She quickly set her purse and keys on a side counter and stepped into his place. "You are not doing all this by yourself."

He glanced at her in surprise and then, with a pleased smile, said, "I figured you'd be too tired."

"I am tired, but this is hardly work."

She quickly finished off the mashed potatoes, put the lid on them and turned to see what was next. He was a little bit behind, but she quickly helped him catch up.

By the time the oven dinged, and he pulled out several pans full of roasted chickens, she realized how much nicer it was to come home and not be by herself but also to have proper meals again. She had let herself go so much in the last eighteen months. It was such a joy to be here and to enjoy real food eaten with a crowd of wonderful people.

Alfred announced dinnertime, while she set up the dining room table. By the time everyone arrived and stepped in to help, Alfred was already bringing out trolleys of food.

After dinner was served, Ice asked, "Bailey, how was your first day back?"

"Overworked, underpaid and lonely."

There was silence as everyone looked at her. She gave a sheepish grin. "I said I worked alone. I have an office where no one stops by. Nobody knew I was missing, and I had several angry emails and angry phone calls, because the people who sent orders by email without getting a confirmation from me had assumed I'd taken care of everything. But I was gone for the week, and nobody even knew."

More silence.

Rhodes said, "That's not good."

"Well, it was good for a long time. But it felt kind of strange going back there today."

"And then you would have just gone home to an empty apartment, right?" Sienna asked.

Bailey nodded. "It was kind of an eye-opener to see how much I had isolated and insulated myself from the rest of the world, by picking a job where I never saw anybody else and by living alone in a place where I didn't know any of my neighbors." She gazed around the table and smiled. "I know more about you guys already than I know about anybody at work or in my apartment building, and I've only known you all for one week."

She caught Ice and Levi exchanging glances. She didn't understand what was going on, but she decided to ignore them. She quickly finished her meal and sat back. "I have to admit it was a pretty exhausting day."

"Time to go rest," Ice said firmly. "We can get the dishes done."

Too tired to argue, Bailey slowly got to her feet, grabbed her purse and keys from the kitchen, made her way through the dining room again and headed for the elevator. When the doors opened, she stepped in and punched the second floor.

Just as the door was about to close, Dakota joined her. She looked at him and smiled. He opened his arms, and she stepped into them. He might want to just be friends, but she was pretty damn glad to have him in her life in any capacity. He hugged her close.

When the door opened, he walked with her to her room. "You don't have to hide away in your room, you know, just because you're tired. There is a TV room, a living room and other lounges."

She nodded. "But it still feels like I'm a guest, so …"

"You are a guest, but you aren't a guest. You're filling a unique role here now," he said with a big grin.

"I forgot to ask at dinnertime. Any updates?" She wandered into her room, tossed her purse and keys on her bed and sat down on the edge. She shifted to the headboard with the propped up pillows and tried to get comfortable while she waited for him to answer.

"Both men are talking to the police. The mayor was hurt pretty badly. They will be charged, and we're certain the mayor won't be the mayor again."

She nodded. "Lots of death. But in a way, there's so much life here too." She glanced at Dakota. "I definitely have friends here."

He gave her that special smile that had surprised her when she'd first seen it because it made her heart race, something she hadn't felt in so long. She stretched her legs and said, "We're friends, right?"

He nodded. "Yes, of course."

"There's no *of course*," she said. "I'm trying to figure out what our relationship is."

"Friends," he said in confusion. "What were you thinking we were?"

Remembering Ice's words of wisdom, she took a deep breath. "I was hoping we were more than friends."

He sat down on the bed beside her and patted her on the leg. She knew he didn't mean it in any kind of demeaning way, but it was a friendly pat when she wanted so much more.

She sighed. "We're really only friends, aren't we?"

"No," he said in confusion. "I don't understand."

She turned to look at him and smiled. "I'll tell you what. You give me a proper kiss, and then we'll know."

He reared back and asked cautiously, "Kiss you?" He frowned, assessing the abrupt change in her demeanor. "I know you're still getting over your husband. I didn't want to push it," he said honestly.

"I've been getting over my husband for a long time. The fact is, I got over him a long time ago."

He looked at her. "If you're sure."

But she could tell he didn't believe her. "You still haven't kissed me."

He chuckled, wrapped her up gently in his arms and gave her a kiss. It wasn't passionate, but it was more than friendly. When he lifted his head, he said, "Have a good night." He got up and walked out.

She stared at the door as it closed and groaned. "Well, that was a strikeout."

She thought about it for the rest of the evening, and the next morning she got up and didn't see him until she left for work. He stood outside her car, waiting for her. "I can drive myself now," she said, pointing to her vehicle.

He nodded but tilted her chin up and gave her another kiss. It felt the same as the one the night before ... no passion, just a loving kindness. Maybe he was scared. That thought surprised her but delighted her too; she smiled good-bye and headed into work.

And she followed that routine for the next few days.

She didn't understand what to do or how to make him realize she was ready for more.

By the time Friday night rolled around, several of the gang had returned, and she was inundated with more strangers. There were lots of long looks shared between partners—some took off for the weekend; some stuck around for a bit, then disappeared. Dakota asked if she wanted to watch a movie.

She thought about it and nodded. "Sure."

About eight of them watched a movie in the big living room. When it was done, she headed up toward her room. Things were still odd here.

Ice promised Bailey that she could stay until she made it to her doctor's appointment. The trouble was, she hadn't any thoughts as to where she would move after this. She had to find another place to live, and she just hadn't done anything about it.

Because she didn't want to. She wanted to stay here. Ice also hadn't brought up any more suggestions about a job with Alfred. Bailey didn't know if Ice had just been testing the waters or had been joking.

Bailey went to her room, leaving the door open, and just propped herself up on her bed with her tablet. Trouble was, she was restless. She wanted so much more from Dakota than he was willing to give. More than he thought she was willing to give.

Communication was the key to everything. Part of the reason she hadn't looked for an apartment was because she wanted to stay here, and the reason she wanted to stay here was because of Dakota. Knowing that the doctor's office was open on Saturday and that she would get her stitches out then, she also knew she had no more excuses or reasons not to move out. It was time for her and Dakota to talk.

She got up and knocked on his door. At his call to come in, she turned the knob and entered.

He was on his laptop behind a small desk. He turned to glance at her. "Hey."

Friendly, unassuming and not pushy. She walked over and stood right beside him, grasped either side of his face, bent down and kissed him with all the passion she'd kept bottled up inside, searching for a response, needing to know if anything was between them. She'd never known anybody with such self-control, and, if that was what it was, then that was fine because she would destroy it in a big way. But, if nothing was between them, that was a whole different story. When she came up for air, he stared at her, a glazed look in his eyes.

All he murmured was, "More."

She chuckled, lowered her head and kissed him again. She stroked her hands through his scalp, softly massaging as she gently explored his mouth, her tongue tangling with his, and yet he didn't put his arms around her or hold her in any way. When she lifted her head the second time and stepped back, he stared at her. She could see the passion clouding his gaze.

"So why, if you felt like that," he whispered, "haven't you let me know before now?"

"I tried to," she said earnestly. "But it seemed like you were always holding me at arm's length."

He stood up and held her in his arms carefully. "Because of your husband. Because of your back. Because your life was a mess and you were attacked."

She reared back to stare up at him. "And none of that had anything to do with you."

The smile dawned in the back of his eyes, and he whispered, "No, just the rescuing part."

"All heroes are supposed to rescue damsels in distress."

He chuckled. "I'm not hero material."

"You absolutely are," she whispered. "This is the band of

heroes here. I can't believe how many men—good men—live in this place."

"Any man in particular?" he asked with a mock glare in his eyes.

She chuckled. "Just one."

"Which one?" he asked, but this time his eyes were twinkling.

"Oh, no you don't," she said. She slowly disentangled her arms and stepped back.

He reached out to grab her gently. "You still have stitches."

"Are you telling me that you can't figure out how to make that work for us?" She shook her head in amusement. "And here I thought you guys were the best of the best."

She didn't make it to the door before he was there, his arms wrapped around her, holding her close against his chest. From his erection prodding against her pelvis to her breasts flattened against his chest, he held her tight.

"I was waiting to make sure you had healed."

She chuckled. "That's nice. I've healed in so many ways. If my back needs an extra day or two to catch up, that doesn't matter either."

He lowered his head and whispered, "Are you sure?"

She whispered back, "Yes."

She didn't think she'd have to coax him into bed. Once he had determined that her husband was no longer an issue, he was right there.

Within moments she found herself wearing only the bandage on her back. She looked down in surprise. "How the hell did you do that?"

His chuckle was low and deep as he quickly divested himself of his clothing. "Remember, I'm the best of the best." He arched his eyebrows at her.

She smiled, walked over to his bed and flipped back the covers on both sides. As he walked toward her, she glanced at him. "Prove it."

And with a laugh he pulled her with him to the bed. And there followed one of the most enjoyable hours of her life. Just the sheer enjoyment of knowing they could be together, spend time together like this, exploring each other's bodies, caressing, hugging, touching—it was extraordinary.

She found herself unexpectedly greedy. Unable to stop touching, tasting. She'd never thought she'd want another man as she had her husband. Never thought to feel the sensations rippling through her heart and soul. For a long time she'd been afraid her life was over. That there'd be no recovery. No future. She'd finally realized something would of course be down the road for her, but the exact nature had always been dark, dismal.

Now life opened up with hope. Joy.

Tears burned in the corner of her eyes, but, instead of wiping them away, she embraced them, letting them pour because they were no longer tears of pain but of letting go. Saying good-bye. And a rejoicing of being where she was now, finally at this point in her future.

"You okay?" Dakota murmured from above her, easing off her overheated skin.

Instinctively she reached up, wrapping her arms around his neck to hold him tight. "Never better."

He gazed down at her, worry lurking in the dark depths of his eyes.

She smiled up at him. "Tears of joy. I never thought to feel this way about another man. You are so very special."

A light burned bright, taking over his face. He lowered

his head, his passion finding a matching flame inside her. Within seconds they were consumed by that fire.

She switched positions and rose over him to slowly lower herself on his erection. Fully seated, she stopped, gasping as shudders of perfection rippled up and down her spine. She tilted her head and arched her back. She stopped and gasped again.

"You okay?" he asked, his voice thick, guttural.

She nodded, her eyes closed, her face toward the ceiling. "It's just been so long."

His hand slid up her hips, and he held her firm as he whispered, "Good."

She chuckled, leaned over, and, using his shoulders as a brace, picked up her tempo, taking them both to a home run.

When she collapsed back down again, he wrapped his arms around her tightly. "If you're sore tomorrow, the doctor will be upset," he warned.

"I'll tell him exactly what caused the damage. I'm sure he'll understand," she said quietly.

He froze for a long moment and then chuckled. "Yeah, I guess he would."

WHEN DAKOTA WALKED her into the doctor's office the next morning, it was strange and yet comforting. They held hands the whole time they waited, as if they couldn't get close enough. He didn't want to let go of her.

When she was inside the exam room and sitting on the table with her shirt up to let the doctor check her over, Dakota paced the small room.

The doctor glanced at him. "What's the worry?"

"Her back okay?" Dakota demanded.

The doctor looked at him in surprise, glanced down at the stitches and said, "It looks fine. I'm taking out the last of them right now."

Bailey chuckled. "He was worried our lovemaking may have hurt my back."

"I'm sure he took good care of you, and it's a good sign he's worried about you," the doctor said comfortably. He quickly finished the job, added some antibacterial ointment. "Do you need another bandage on this?"

Bailey shook her head. "No, thank you." When the doctor was done, Dakota and Bailey walked back outside. "See? You worry too much."

He grabbed her and held her close. "For you, I will always worry. Because I don't want to spend another day without you. You're the best thing that ever happened to me."

She froze, looked up at him and gave him such a beautiful smile that he could feel his heart sigh on the inside. He hadn't realized how much he'd been missing having somebody like her in his life. No, not like her. There was nobody like her. She was so damn special.

"Hardly," she said with a half laugh, making him realize he'd made the last comment out loud.

He bent and kissed the tip of her nose. "So special."

She wrapped her arm through his. "Show me."

"When we get home," he said. "There I'll be happy to show you how perfect you are. We are … forever."

She looked up, suddenly serious. "Promise?"

He lowered his head, and, just as his lips whispered against hers, he said. "I promise."

Epilogue

MICHAEL SHOOK HIS head at Levi's persuasive argument. "I'm not ready," he said quietly. "Honestly, Levi, I might never be ready."

"Take your time. It's an adjustment for all of us. There's no right or wrong way. Just take the time you need. Then when you're ready, call me. I'll have a job for you."

Michael ended the call and slipped his phone into his pocket. He knew Levi meant well. He was a hell of a team player and never left a man behind. Technically Michael wasn't one of Levi's men, but they were on the same side. Different SEAL units yet had been on missions together. For both Michael and Levi that was enough. They belonged to a special brotherhood. And neither would ever forget that.

But Michael wasn't sure he wanted to go back to the same line of work as they'd done in the military. He'd gotten out, and he wanted to stay out.

He understood Levi's arguments about how much good they could do and that Michael had skills they needed. He understood it all, but he was sick inside. Sick of the ways in which people could hurt each other. The darkness on a global scale. So much ugliness was out there, and he'd been a part of it for so long … until he couldn't do it anymore. And he'd walked away.

It would take something major for him to step back into

the game. He was afraid, if he ever took that step, he'd never leave again. He didn't want to walk in darkness forever.

At one point he'd hoped for a wife and children. For a normal life. Whatever the hell that meant.

For a long time he'd pushed that life off as being something intended for men who didn't deal in violence every day of their lives.

When he'd become a civilian, it had taken months for that old dream to resurface. He hated to let it go again.

But there was no doubt that, if the right call to action came, he'd go willingly. He'd put that dream on the back burner again. Although he wouldn't do it for anyone, but, if there was the right cry for help, he'd step in and answer.

He could do no less.

But, until then, he would stay here and work on creating that normal life.

This concludes Book 9 of Heroes for Hire: Dakota's Delight.

Read about Michael's Mercy: Heroes for Hire, Book 10

Heroes for Hire: Michael's Mercy (Book #10)

The Sleeper SEALs are former US Navy SEALs recruited by a new CIA counterterrorism division to handle solo dark-op missions to combat terrorism on US soil.

When things go bad in Michael's world, things go horribly, terrifyingly bad.

It's been one year since hardened Navy SEAL Michael Hampton walked away from his career. He never thought to return, but then his former commander called with the news that an old friend was murdered while undercover—and the commander needs Michael's help.

Knowing the next dead body might be his, Michael takes his friend's place at the home of man bankrolling a terrorist cell. Michael's official mission is to find out all he can to bring down the man's operation. Michael's personal mission is to find out who murdered his friend.

Mercy got the maid job that her sister had last held— just before she was murdered. With the police lacking leads and persons-of-interest, Mercy decides it's up to her to find out what happened. Inside the huge home, she meets Michael and becomes immediately suspicious ... and immediately attracted.

When their paths cross, she realizes he's not who he seems either.

Can they each find the truth about their objectives and

about themselves? Or will the terrorists' money man get wind of the traitors in his midst and take care of them before they can take care of him?

Each story in this multiauthor-branded series is a standalone novel, and the series can be read in any order.

Welcome to *Michael's Mercy*, Book 10 in the Heroes for Hire series, reconnecting readers with the unforgettable men from SEALs of Honor in a new series of action-packed, page-turning romantic suspense that fans have come to expect from USA TODAY best-selling author Dale Mayer. This book is part of the continuity series Sleeper SEALS (Book 3).

Book 10 is available now!

To find out more visit Dale Mayer's website.

https://geni.us/DMMichaelUniversal

Other Military Series by Dale Mayer

SEALs of Honor

Heroes for Hire

SEALs of Steel

The K9 Files

The Mavericks

Bullards Battle

Hathaway House

Terkel's Team

Ryland's Reach: Bullard's Battle (Book #1)

Welcome to a new stand-alone but interconnected series from Dale Mayer. This is Bullard's story—and that of his team's. All raw, rough, incredibly capable men who have one goal: to find out who was behind the attack on their leader, before the attacker, or attackers, return to finish the job.

Stay tuned for more nonstop action as the men narrow down their suspects ... and find a way to let love back into their own empty lives.

His rescue from the ocean after a horrible plane explosion was his top priority, in any way, shape, or form. A small sailboat and a nurse to do the job was more than Ryland hoped for.

When Tabi somehow drags him and his buddy Garret onboard and surprisingly gets them to a naval ship close by, Ryland figures he'd used up all his luck and his friend's too. Sure enough, those who attacked the plane they were in weren't content to let him slowly die in the ocean. No. Surviving had made him a target all over again.

Tabi isn't expecting her sailing holiday to include the rescue of two badly injured men and then to end with the loss of her beloved sailboat. Her instincts save them, but now she finds it tough to let them go—even as more of Bullard's team members come to them—until it becomes apparent that not only are Bullard and his men still targets ... but she is too.

B ULLARD CHECKED THAT the helicopter was loaded with their bags and that his men were ready to leave.

He walked back one more time, his gaze on Ice. She'd never looked happier, never looked more perfect. His heart ached, but he knew she remained a caring friend and always would be. He opened his arms; she ran into them, and he held her close, whispering, "The offer still stands."

She leaned back and smiled up at him. "Maybe if and when Levi's been gone for a long enough time for me to forget," she said in all seriousness.

"That's not happening. You two, now three, will live long and happy lives together," he said, smiling down at the woman knew to be the most beautiful, inside and out. She would never be his, but he always kept a little corner of his heart open and available, in case she wanted to surprise him and to slide inside.

And then he realized she'd already been a part of his heart all this time. That was a good ten to fifteen years by now. But she kept herself in the friend category, and he understood because she and Levi, partners and now parents, were perfect together.

Bullard reached out and shook Levi's hand. "It was a hell of a blast," he said. "When you guys do a big splash, you really do a *big* splash."

Ice laughed. "A few days at home sounds perfect for me now."

"It looks great," he said, his hands on his hips as he surveyed the people in the massive pool surrounded by the palm trees, all designed and decked out by Ice. Right beside all the war machines that he heartily approved of. He grinned at her. "When are you coming over to visit?" His gaze went to Levi, raising his eyebrows back at her. "You guys should come over for a week or two or three."

"It's not a bad idea," Levi said. "We could use a long holiday, just not yet."

"That sounds familiar." Bullard grinned. "Anyway, I'm off. We'll hit the airport and then pick up the plane and head home." He added, "As always, call if you need me."

Everybody raised a hand as he returned to the helicopter and his buddy who was flying him to the airport. Ice had volunteered to shuttle him there, but he hadn't wanted to take her away from her family or to prolong the goodbye. He hopped inside, waving at everybody as the helicopter lifted. Two of his men, Ryland and Garret, were in the back seats. They always traveled with him.

Bullard would pick up the rest of his men in Australia. He stared down at the compound as he flew overhead. He preferred his compound at home, but damn they'd done a nice job here.

With everybody on the ground screaming goodbye, Bullard sailed over Houston, heading toward the airport. His two men never said a word. They all knew how he felt about Ice. But not one of them would cross that line and say anything. At least not if they expected to still have jobs.

It was one thing to fall in love with another man's woman, but another thing to fall in love with a woman who was so unique, so different, and so absolutely perfect that you knew, just knew, there was no hope of finding anybody else like her. But she and Levi had been together way before Bullard had ever met her, which made it that much more heartbreaking.

Still, he'd turned and looked forward. He had a full roster of jobs himself to focus on when he got home. Part of him was tired of the life; another part of him couldn't wait to head out on the next adventure. He managed to run everything from his command centers in one or two of his locations. He'd spent a lot of time and effort at the second one and kept a full team at both locations, yet preferred to spend most of his time at the old one. It felt more like home to him, and he'd like to be there now, but still had many more days before that could happen.

The helicopter lowered to the tarmac, he stepped out, said his goodbyes and walked across to where his private plane waited. It was one of the things that he loved, being a pilot of both helicopters and airplanes, and owning both birds himself.

That again was another way he and Ice were part of the same team, of the same mind-set. He'd been looking for another woman like Ice for himself, but no such luck. Sure, lots were around for short-term relationships, but most of them couldn't handle his lifestyle or the violence of the world that he lived in. He understood that.

The ones who did had a hard edge to them that he found difficult to live with. Bullard appreciated everybody's being alert and aware, but if there wasn't some softness in the women, they seemed to turn cold all the way through.

As he boarded his small plane, Ryland and Garret following behind, Bullard called out in his loud voice, "Let's go, slow pokes. We've got a long flight ahead of us."

The men grinned, confident Bullard was teasing, as was his usual routine during their off-hours.

"Well, we're ready, not sure about you though ..." Ryland said, smirking.

"We're waiting on you this time," Garret added with a chuckle. "Good thing you're the boss."

Bullard grinned at his two right-hand men. "Isn't that the truth?" He dropped his bags at one of the guys' feet and said, "Stow all this stuff, will you? I want to get our flight path cleared and get the hell out of here."

They'd all enjoyed the break. He tried to get over once a year to visit Ice and Levi and same in reverse. But it was time to get back to business. He started up the engines, got confirmation from the tower. They were heading to Australia for this next job. He really wanted to go straight back to Africa, but it would be a while yet. They'd refuel in Honolulu.

Ryland came in and sat down in the copilot's spot, buckled in, then asked, "You ready?"

Bullard laughed. "When have you ever known me *not* to be ready?" At that, he taxied down the runway. Before long he was up in the air, at cruising level, and heading to Hawaii. "Gotta love these views from up here," Bullard said. "This place is magical."

"It is once you get up above all the smog," he said. "Why Australia again?"

"Remember how we were supposed to check out that newest compound in Australia that I've had my eye on? Besides the alpha team is coming off that ugly job in Sydney. We'll give them a day or two of R&R then head home."

"Right. We could have some equally ugly payback on that job."

Bullard shrugged. "That goes for most of our jobs. It's the life."

"And don't you have enough compounds to look after?"

"Yes I do, but that kid in me still looks to take over the world. Just remember that."

"Better you go home to Africa and look after your first two compounds," Ryland said.

"Maybe," Bullard admitted. "But it seems hard to not continue expanding."

"You need a partner," Ryland said abruptly. "That might ease the savage beast inside. Keep you home more."

"Well, the only one I like," he said, "is married to my best friend."

"I'm sorry about that," Ryland said quietly. "What a shit deal."

"No," Bullard said. "I came on the scene last. They were always meant to be together. Especially now they are a family."

"If you say so," Ryland said.

Bullard nodded. "Damn right, I say so."

And that set the tone for the next many hours. They landed in Hawaii, and while they fueled up everybody got off to stretch their legs by walking around outside a bit as this was a small private airstrip, not exactly full of hangars and tourists. Then they hopped back on board again for takeoff.

"I can fly," Ryland offered as they took off.

"We'll switch in a bit," Bullard said. "Surprisingly, I'm doing okay yet, but I'll let you take her down."

"Yeah, it's still a long flight," Ryland said studying the islands below. It was a stunning view of the area.

"I love the islands here. Sometimes I just wonder about the benefit of, you know, crashing into the sea, coming up on a deserted island, and finding the simple life again," Bullard said with a laugh.

"I hear you," Ryland said. "Every once in a while, I wonder the same."

Several hours later Ryland looked up and said abruptly, "We've made good time considering we've already passed Fiji."

Bullard yawned.

"Let's switch."

Bullard smiled, nodded, and said, "Fine. I'll hand it over to you."

Just then a funny noise came from the engine on the right side.

They looked at each other, and Ryland said, "Uh-oh. That's not good news."

Boom!

And the plane exploded.

Find Bullard's Battle (Book #1) here!

To find out more visit Dale Mayer's website.

https://geni.us/DMRylandUniversal

Damon's Deal: Terkel's Team (Book #1)

Welcome to a brand-new connected series of intrigue, betrayal, and ... murder, from the *USA Today* best-selling author Dale Mayer. A series with all the elements you've come to love, plus so much more... including psychics!

A betrayal from within has Terkel frantic to protect those he can, as his team falls one by one, from a murderous killer he helped create.

I CE POURED HERSELF a coffee and sat down at the compound's massive dining room table with the others. When her phone rang, she smiled at the number displayed. "Hey, Terk. How're you doing?" She put the call on Speakerphone.

"I'm okay," Terkel said, his voice distracted and tight.

"Terk?" Merk called from across the table. He got up and walked closer and sat across from Levi. "You don't sound too good, brother. What's up?"

"I'm fine," Terk said. "Or I will be. Right now, things are blown to shit."

"As in literally?" Merk asked.

"The entire group," Terk said, "they're all gone. I had a solid team of eight, and they're all gone."

"Dead?"

Several others stood to join them, gathered around Ice's phone. Levi stepped forward, his hand on Ice's shoulder. "Terk? Are they all dead?"

"No." Terk took a deep breath. "I'm not making sense. I'm sorry."

"Take it easy," Ice said, her voice calm and reassuring. "What do you mean, *they're all gone?*"

"All their abilities are gone," he said. "Something's happened to them. Somebody has deliberately removed whatever super senses they could utilize—or what we have been utilizing for the last ten years for the government." His tone was bitter. "When the US gov recently closed us down, they promised that our black ops department would never rise again, but I didn't expect them to attack us personally."

"What are you talking about?" Merk said in alarm, standing up now to stare at Ice's phone. "Are you in danger?"

"Maybe? I don't know," Terk said. "I need to find out exactly what the hell's going on."

"What can we do to help?" Ice asked.

Terk gave a broken laugh. "That's not why I'm calling. Well, it is, but it isn't."

Ice looked at Merk, who frowned, as he shook his head. Ice knew he and the others had heard Terk's stressed out tone and the completely confusing bits and pieces coming from his mouth. Ice said, "Terk, you're not making sense again. Take a breath and explain. Please. You're scaring me."

Terk took a long slow deep breath. "Tell Stone to open the gate," he said. "She's out there."

"Who's out there?" Levi asked, hopped up, looked outside, and shrugged.

"She's coming up the road now. You have to let her in."

"Who? Why?"

"*Because*," he said, "she's also harnessed with C-4."

"Jesus," Levi said, bolting to display the camera feeds to the big screen in the room. "Is it live?"

"It is, and she's been sent to you."

"Well, that's an interesting move," Ice said, her voice sharp, activating her comm to connect to Stone in the control room. "Who's after us?"

"I think it's rebels within the Iranian government. But it could be our own government. I don't know anymore," Terk snapped. "I also don't know how they got her so close to you. Or how they pinned your connection to me," he said. "I've been very careful."

"We can look after ourselves," Ice said immediately. "But who is this woman to you?"

"She's pregnant," he said, "so that adds to the intensity here."

"Understood. So who is the father? Is he connected somehow?"

There was silence on the other end.

Merk said, "Terk, talk to us."

"She's carrying my baby," Terk replied, his voice heavy.

Merk, his expression grim, looked at Ice, her face mirroring his shock. He asked, "How do you know her, Terk?"

"Brother, you don't understand," Terk said. "I've never met this woman before in my life." And, with that, the phone went dead.

Find Terkel's Team (Book #1) here!

To find out more visit Dale Mayer's website.

https://geni.us/DMTTDamonUniversal

Author's Note

Thank you for reading Dakota's Delight: Heroes for Hire, Book 9! If you enjoyed the book, please take a moment and leave a short review.

Dear reader,

I love to hear from readers, and you can contact me at my website: www.dalemayer.com or at my Facebook author page. To be informed of new releases and special offers, sign up for my newsletter or follow me on BookBub. And if you are interested in joining Dale Mayer's Reader Group, here is the Facebook sign up page.
http://geni.us/DaleMayerFBGroup

Cheers,
Dale Mayer

About the Author

Dale Mayer is a *USA Today* best-selling author, best known for her SEALs military romances, her Psychic Visions series, and her Lovely Lethal Garden cozy series. Her contemporary romances are raw and full of passion and emotion (Broken But … Mending, Hathaway House series). Her thrillers will keep you guessing (Kate Morgan, By Death series), and her romantic comedies will keep you giggling (*It's a Dog's Life*, a stand-alone novella; and the Broken Protocols series, starring Charming Marvin, the cat).

Dale honors the stories that come to her—and some of them are crazy, break all the rules and cross multiple genres!

To go with her fiction, she also writes nonfiction in many different fields, with books available on résumé writing, companion gardening, and the US mortgage system. All her books are available in print and ebook format.

Connect with Dale Mayer Online

Dale's Website – www.dalemayer.com
Twitter – @DaleMayer
Facebook Page – geni.us/DaleMayerFBFanPage
Facebook Group – geni.us/DaleMayerFBGroup
BookBub – geni.us/DaleMayerBookbub
Instagram – geni.us/DaleMayerInstagram
Goodreads – geni.us/DaleMayerGoodreads
Newsletter – geni.us/DaleNews

Also by Dale Mayer

Published Adult Books:

Bullard's Battle
Ryland's Reach, Book 1
Cain's Cross, Book 2
Eton's Escape, Book 3
Garret's Gambit, Book 4
Kano's Keep, Book 5
Fallon's Flaw, Book 6
Quinn's Quest, Book 7
Bullard's Beauty, Book 8
Bullard's Best, Book 9

Terkel's Team
Damon's Deal, Book 1

Kate Morgan
Simon Says… Hide, Book 1

Hathaway House
Aaron, Book 1
Brock, Book 2
Cole, Book 3
Denton, Book 4

The K9 Files

Psychic Vision Series

Tuesday's Child

Hide 'n Go Seek

Maddy's Floor

Garden of Sorrow

Knock Knock…

Rare Find

Eyes to the Soul

Now You See Her

Shattered

Into the Abyss

Seeds of Malice

Eye of the Falcon

Itsy-Bitsy Spider

Unmasked

Deep Beneath

From the Ashes

Stroke of Death

Ice Maiden

Snap, Crackle…

Psychic Visions Books 1–3

Psychic Visions Books 4–6

Psychic Visions Books 7–9

By Death Series

Touched by Death

Haunted by Death

Chilled by Death

By Death Books 1–3

Broken Protocols – Romantic Comedy Series

Cat's Meow

Cat's Pajamas

Cat's Cradle

Cat's Claus

Broken Protocols 1-4

Broken and... Mending

Skin

Scars

Scales (of Justice)

Broken but... Mending 1-3

Glory

Genesis

Tori

Celeste

Glory Trilogy

Biker Blues

Morgan: Biker Blues, Volume 1

Cash: Biker Blues, Volume 2

SEALs of Honor

Mason: SEALs of Honor, Book 1

Hawk: SEALs of Honor, Book 2

Dane: SEALs of Honor, Book 3

Swede: SEALs of Honor, Book 4

Shadow: SEALs of Honor, Book 5

Cooper: SEALs of Honor, Book 6

Heroes for Hire

Heroes for Hire, Books 10–12

Heroes for Hire, Books 13–15

SEALs of Steel

Badger: SEALs of Steel, Book 1

Erick: SEALs of Steel, Book 2

Cade: SEALs of Steel, Book 3

Talon: SEALs of Steel, Book 4

Laszlo: SEALs of Steel, Book 5

Geir: SEALs of Steel, Book 6

Jager: SEALs of Steel, Book 7

The Final Reveal: SEALs of Steel, Book 8

SEALs of Steel, Books 1–4

SEALs of Steel, Books 5–8

SEALs of Steel, Books 1–8

The Mavericks

Kerrick, Book 1

Griffin, Book 2

Jax, Book 3

Beau, Book 4

Asher, Book 5

Ryker, Book 6

Miles, Book 7

Nico, Book 8

Keane, Book 9

Lennox, Book 10

Gavin, Book 11

Shane, Book 12

Diesel, Book 13

Jerricho, Book 14

The Mavericks, Books 1–2

The Mavericks, Books 3–4

The Mavericks, Books 5–6

The Mavericks, Books 7–8

The Mavericks, Books 9–10

The Mavericks, Books 11–12

Collections

Dare to Be You…

Dare to Love…

Dare to be Strong…

RomanceX3

Standalone Novellas

It's a Dog's Life

Riana's Revenge

Second Chances

Published Young Adult Books:

Family Blood Ties Series

Vampire in Denial

Vampire in Distress

Vampire in Design

Vampire in Deceit

Vampire in Defiance

Vampire in Conflict

Vampire in Chaos

Vampire in Crisis

Vampire in Control

Vampire in Charge

Family Blood Ties Set 1–3

Family Blood Ties Set 1–5

Family Blood Ties Set 4–6

Family Blood Ties Set 7–9

Sian's Solution, A Family Blood Ties Series Prequel
Novelette

Design series

Dangerous Designs

Deadly Designs

Darkest Designs

Design Series Trilogy

Standalone

In Cassie's Corner

Gem Stone (a Gemma Stone Mystery)

Time Thieves

Published Non-Fiction Books:

Career Essentials

Career Essentials: The Résumé

Career Essentials: The Cover Letter

Career Essentials: The Interview

Career Essentials: 3 in 1

www.ingramcontent.com/pod-product-compliance
Lightning Source LLC
Chambersburg PA
CBHW071516110726
47908CB00003B/858